A LANCASTER

FAMILY

Christmas

KATE LLOYD

UNION BAY
PUBLISHING

Praise for
KATE LLOYD'S AMISH FICTION

Leaving Lancaster:

"This talented and capable writer will leave you wanting more."

Suzanne Woods Fisher,

bestselling author of *A Season on the Wind*

Pennsylvania Patchwork:

"Readers of Amish fiction will love every moment."

Hillary Manton Lodge, author of *Jane of Austin*

A Letter from Lancaster County:

"Anyone who picks up a novel by Kate Lloyd is in for a treat."

Shelley Shepard Gray,

bestselling author of *A Perfect Christmas Romance*

A Letter from Lancaster County:

"Everything I want in a book. Highly recommended."

Beth Wiseman,

bestselling author of *An Unlikely Match*

Starting from Scratch:

"This is a story rich with details from the Lancaster County Amish countryside."

Kelly Irvin,

bestselling author of *The Amish of Sky County*

To Connie Lynch

CHAPTER 1

I FELT A FAMILIAR finger jab my shoulder.
"Diana, are we keeping you awake?" my boss
asked me, his voice peeved.

Around us, the Metropolitan Art Museum's gift
store swirled with activity and color, boisterous
holiday shoppers exploring the calendars, books,
lavish silk scarves, facsimiles of ancient artifacts,
tree ornaments, and prints on the walls. Squirrelly
preschool-aged kids circled their mothers' legs and
argued over who wanted what, but the man in front
of me paid them little heed.

"Oh." I jerked and blinked. "I'm very sorry,
Mr. Simonton. I didn't sleep well last night." My
parents' yelling at each other had jarred into my
slumber like jackhammers until I'd heard the door

to our apartment slam. This morning Dad was gone. Again.

The corners of Mr. Simonton's mouth angled down. "Wasn't fatigue your excuse last week for running late, Miss Manzella?"

Behind him I could see Betsy Yoder, my friend and coworker, stifling a smirk. He turned and lowered his eyebrows at her until she spun away to straighten a display of Egyptian replica earrings on the glass counter.

"It won't happen again," I told him, raking my hand through my brown, shoulder-length hair and trying to regain my composure.

"You're darned right it won't." His severe mouth moved closer to my ear. "I don't care if your mother is on the museum's board of trustees. I won't tolerate your lackadaisical work ethic, understand?" He snickered. "From what I hear, she won't be on the board for much longer."

"But—" I cringed, knowing that the tabloids had been airing my parents' dirty laundry for months. Their upcoming divorce was going to be fierce and ugly, and it would be all over the cheap tabloids, the kind at corner grocery checkouts. I'd quit reading them.

The truth was, my mother would be more crushed to lose her position on the museum's board of trustees than to lose her husband. Which, it appeared, she had. My father couldn't care less what she thought of him and had laughed at her when she'd begged him to go to counseling with her last month.

"Very sorry, Mr. Simonton," I said. "I'll get busy right away." I scanned the table full of Christmas cards and recalled my assignment. As if I hadn't skipped a beat, I started to arrange the table, moving the cards that said *Happy Holidays* to the front section. Anything that said *Merry Christmas*, I pushed to the back. Get me away from that religious stuff. There was a time I believed, but no more. Thanks to a boatload of bitter disappointments, including my parents, I'd learned that the only thing I could depend on was myself and my cutie-pie cairn terrier, Piper.

I plastered a smile on my face and glanced up at Mr. Simonton. "Is this what you had in mind?" I asked.

"Better, I guess." He straightened several boxes, as if the customers wouldn't mess them up in three minutes. "But isn't that the exact display you put together last year?"

"How kind of you to remember." I forced my mouth to curve into a perky smile.

"We need something completely different," he said. "Christmas is a little more than a week away, and we're overstocked."

I hoped that firing me on the spot wasn't the kind of difference he had in mind. Not that I didn't long for a complete change. Mom had arranged this job for me three years ago, and everyone here knew it. "Poor little rich girl," some called me behind my back, even though I put in as many hours as everyone else.

But they were right. I was spoiled. I lived in a deluxe apartment with my parents on Central Park East. It was primo property on the seventh floor, with a splendid view of the park and just a short walk to work. At twenty-nine I knew it was time to move out, but I couldn't afford to pay rent on an apartment, let alone the extra damage deposit required for owning a pet. I couldn't live without Piper. She needed my attention and was always ecstatic to see me.

"What did you have in mind?" I asked, forcing the corners of my mouth to stay up.

"Figure out something yourself," Mr. Simonton said. "Don't rely on me for everything."

Betsy bounced over to us. "Need more merchandise?" She and I couldn't look more different, what with her willowy stature and long mane of blond hair pulled back into a French roll. Next to her I was a shrimp.

Mr. Simonton let out a huff. "Betsy, if you're going to suggest Amish and Mennonite knickknacks this time of year when I'm trying to clear out stock, no need. Anyway, this is a prestigious art museum."

"The Amish and Mennonites craft beautiful quilts and dolls," she shot back. "We could do a special exhibit and sell a ton of them."

Betsy ran a business on the side, selling to-die-for Amish dolls and Mennonite quilts and table runners she acquired wholesale through her relatives and their neighbors in Lancaster County, Pennsylvania. She said anything Amish or Mennonite seemed to sell, though I hadn't bought from her myself. I loved the look, but it wouldn't suit my parents' sleek ultramodern apartment.

"That won't be necessary," he said, backstepping away from her.

"Thanks for saving me," I told her when he was out of earshot. "I was sure he was going to sack me."

"Nah." Her lavender flowered dress hung midcalf. "This time of year? We're already low on employees."

"Wait until January," I said, feeling deflated. "I'll be ancient history."

"Hey, I have a fun idea that will perk you up," she said. "I'm driving to my folks' house after work to pick up a few last-minute holiday orders. I'll stay for a couple days. You could come with me." I shook my head, but she persisted. "You won't regret it."

Tomorrow and the next were my days off, but I still tried to squirm out of going. Betsy had asked me to accompany her to her parents' home several times before, but I'd always found an excuse not to go. I was a city girl through and through. "There's a nasty cold front moving in tonight according to the weatherman."

"So what? Come on, girlfriend. It'll be an adventure."

"A big, bad cold front," I said. "Temperatures dropping below freezing, and a ton of snow."

"I'll borrow my cousin's four-wheel-drive sedan. She owes me a favor."

I considered her invitation. I wouldn't mind escaping my parents' reality show for a couple of days. According to the tabloids, Dad was hanging out with an opera diva, who was wearing a humongous diamond engagement ring when not on stage, and my mother had been seen a number of times with a hotshot stockbroker. They hadn't gotten along for years, but the idea of a divorce slashed into me like a serrated knife. And while I wished I had a boyfriend to use as an excuse, Vince was a lost cause. He'd dumped me for another woman.

Mr. Simonton was bowing and scraping to a good customer across the room. I decided I needed to get away from him for a couple days, as well as my parents.

"Okay, you're on," I said.

My spine straightened. I'd never wanted to get out of the city before, especially at Christmas, when Manhattan was decked out and at her best. "It's Christmastime in the City" was my favorite holiday song. This year, though, I hadn't even checked out the snazzy windows at Bergdorf Goodman or Macy's. What was wrong with me?

"I'll need to find someone to feed and walk my dog, though," I added. I hated to leave Piper.

"Is she vicious?" she asked in merriment. Betsy had met Piper several times and knew the answer. "Bring the pooch with you. My folks love dogs."

"Don't you have to call and ask for permission to bring an outsider home?" I didn't know much about Betsy's Mennonite background. I pictured a home with an outhouse behind it. Oh dear, not my cup of tea. "Wait, do they have electricity and cell phone reception? Do they have running water? Should I shower before we go?"

"You crack me up. Been reading Amish romance novels?"

"Only one." But the descriptions had stuck in my mind.

"We have all the modern conveniences," she said. "My parents are progressive Mennonites, not Old Order Amish. My folks drive cars, but some Mennonites don't. Like Old Order Mennonites, who still use horse and buggies. On top of that, the Amish call anyone who isn't Amish *English*. It's all very complicated and yet simple once you get used to the routine. I'll explain it all to you when we're up there. I promise you won't have to sleep in a barn, although we have one."

I glanced down at my Ferragamo pumps. "But I assume things are more casual."

"Compared to the Big Apple, yes. My best advice is to bring comfortable, warm clothing," she said. "You have any?"

"I've got skiing stuff, but it's been years. Will my down parka work?"

She took hold of my elbow. "Sure. I'll pick up the car, then swing by your folks' place after work to fetch you and Piper."

As soon as my shift ended, I headed home. In the lobby of my family's apartment building, our doorman, Carlos, greeted me. "Come in, pretty lady, before you freeze." Carlos was muscled, and his skin was chestnut brown. He was good looking in every way and flirtatious, but I never flirted back for fear he'd lose his job.

On the seventh floor, Piper met me at the apartment door with sprightly barking and her stubble of a tail wagging. I was the most special person in Piper's world, which brought me great joy, but sometimes also made me feel pathetic.

I shrugged off my camel-colored cashmere coat. "No need to bring that," I said out loud, hanging it in the closet next to one of my mother's fur jackets and a Christian Dior mink.

I dug through my closets and drawers until I found warm, casual clothes. I dressed in jeans, wool socks, and an amber turtleneck sweater that echoed my eyes. I stuffed my suitcase with an extra outfit, as well as long underwear, mittens, a wool knit hat, and my travel makeup case. Not that I'd need to look good lounging around with Betsy and her parents out in the middle of nowhere, but I never traveled without it.

Piper huddled in her basket, looking much like Toto from *The Wizard of Oz*. I scooped her up and said, "Come on, girlie, we're going on an adventure."

CHAPTER 2

I HADN'T BEEN OUT of the city for years. I gaped at the new construction and the traffic on the expressway as Betsy steered her cousin's Subaru like a pro, weaving between cabs, limousines, and other cars. She even leaned on the horn every now and then, making me laugh. It felt good to laugh.

As we followed the sinking sun, I relaxed back into the passenger seat and fell asleep without meaning to, waking up as she exited a ramp.

"Are we already in Pennsylvania?" I asked.

"Yup."

"Oh, look, it's snowing. So pretty." I noticed her windshield wipers were barely keeping up with the accumulation and felt my nervousness returning. "Maybe we should turn around and head back."

"No way. We're almost there." She turned onto a smaller road. "Have a nice nap?"

"I guess. I had the craziest dream." I peered through the dense white curtain. How could she see where to drive?

"Ooh, please tell." She followed the winding road without hesitation. She looked downright confident.

"Just a jumble of images . . ." The closer we got, the more I doubted this trip. "Are you positively sure your parents won't mind a stranger showing up? Did you call them?"

"Yes, silly."

I glanced into the back seat and saw Piper sacked out, her eyes closed. "And there's room enough for me and a dog?" I asked. "We could stay in a hotel."

"No way. We had eight kids in our family. Most of my siblings have houses of their own now. We have plenty of extra bedrooms."

The snow was making me tired again. I yawned; when I opened my eyes, I saw a horse-drawn buggy headed straight at us.

"Careful," I said, panic elevating my voice.

"No worries." She pressed her foot on the brakes and waved as the buggy flew by. "I'm used to it."

"That guy was driving like . . . like a New York City cabdriver," I said.

Betsy chortled and checked her rearview mirror. "He'd appreciate that description. I've known that guy my whole life. He's cute with a capital *C*."

I'd gotten only a brief glimpse of a man wearing a black hat. "You call that cute?"

"If you saw Jesse up close, you might change your mind." She glanced my way. "Unless a new lover boy would get jealous."

I guffawed. "I haven't been out on a date in months, but no way am I riding in a buggy in a snowstorm."

"The Amish are fantastic people. Wait until you meet some."

"If you say so." I realized I sounded like a snob. Because I basically was. Before I could say anything else, Betsy slowed, took a right, and drove up a snowy lane toward a sprawling three-story house.

"Wow, this is your parents' home?"

"Yup."

"Guess I don't need to worry about taking up too much room." I breathed a sigh of relief.

"Not at all," Betsy reassured me again. "It's just my parents, my youngest sister, and oldest brother, Brett. My other siblings live in Florida where it's nice and warm."

"The snow's coming down harder." I glanced up to the swaying evergreen branches. "And the wind has picked up."

"We got here just in time." She cut the engine.

The front porch lights illuminated the snow-flakes like sparkling diamonds.

Thinking of diamonds made me recall Vince. I had been so sure he'd give me a diamond ring last Christmas. We'd walked past Tiffany's and slowed to admire the engagement rings. He'd asked me which style I liked. Then, a few weeks later, he dropped the bomb: he was seeing another woman, who by now probably wore one of those gorgeous diamond rings. I'd seen the joyous couple's photo in the *New York Times* engagement section, announcing a future wedding. That jerk.

My thoughts were brought back to the present when Betsy's car rocked as if it were being scooped up by a giant's hand. Snowflakes swirled. It was hard to see the house anymore.

"Whoa," I said. "What was that?"

"A hefty gust of wind." She set the parking brake.

"Does it always snow like this?" I asked.

"No, hardly ever. But don't be afraid, we'll be okay."

Again, a gust of wind rocked the Subaru as if it were made of papier-mâché. Piper barked. I saw a large figure coming our way.

"A Sasquatch?" I asked.

"In Lancaster County? Don't be crazy." She buttoned her coat, then plunked a crocheted hat atop her head.

I felt something tug on my side of the car and realized a man was attempting to open my door. I unlocked it, and the door opened, allowing frigid air to fill the automobile's interior. I barely kept my balance as I stood. The man took my hand to steady me. Why had I agreed to come?

"My dog is in the back seat," I said to him.

I could hear him let out a huff over the driving snow. "What else did she bring along?" he yelled to Betsy.

Betsy's words sounded blurry. This must be Brett. I wanted no part of their brother-sister spat. I felt like an intruder.

Piper, usually brave, cringed on the back seat. Poor little thing. For a minute I wished I'd left her back at the apartment, but who knew when or if either of my parents would return to take care of her.

A gravelly noise in the driveway filled my ears as the black horse and buggy I'd seen earlier appeared out of the blizzard. Betsy's brother turned to the driver and spoke in a language I couldn't understand, but in a cordial fashion that told me the men knew each other well.

Without warning, the horse reared, spooked by something. Betsy's brother dropped my arm and stepped forward to grab the magnificent animal by its bridle, steadying it. The Amish guy jumped out of his buggy, and the two men led the horse around the side of the house.

I struggled to get back in the car and locked the door out of habit. No way was I going to try to make it up the snowy walkway and steps to the front porch by myself. Piper growled and then belted out a succession of barks. "Come to Mama," I said, and she jumped in my lap.

"They're putting Jesse's horse in our barn." Betsy got back into the driver's seat. Pellets of snow sounded like gravel against the windows as the wind increased. Steam accumulated on the interior of the windshield. "They'll be back, or my dad will come out."

"Could you understand what that Amish guy was saying?"

"*Yah*, it's Pennsylvania Dutch. Jesse lives next door. We grew up together. He's about Brett's age, and he owns the family farm now."

"He owns a whole farm?" Jesse's stature elevated in my eyes, but what kind of a man would drive a buggy in a snowstorm?

"One of the largest farms in the county," she said. "Eighty acres of cornfields." As if reading my mental list of questions, Betsy added, "I can't imagine Jesse brought his favorite thoroughbred out into the storm on purpose, but he's Amish and doesn't have a phone or TV to catch the weather report."

I'd never heard her talk about a man like this. "You have a crush on him?" I asked.

She grinned. "Is it that obvious? But nothing will ever come of it since I'm not Amish."

"Well, that puts me out of the running too." I chuckled, because how impossible would that be?

However Betsy's cheerful expression flattened. "You wouldn't," she said, her voice plaintive.

"No, I promise not to compete with you, over that guy or anything."

CHAPTER 3

A HAND RAPPED ON my window, making me start and Piper bark.

"That's just Brett," Betsy said.

"He scared me half to death." I unlocked the door again as he grappled with the handle, and shivered as an icy gust blasted against me. Brett was twice my size, thank goodness, or we'd both be blown away. Still, I hesitated to go back into the cold until he yelled, "Do you want to spend the night out here?"

Was he ridiculing me?

"Go with him," Betsy said, giggling.

Brett took my hand as I stood, then circled his arm around my waist to stabilize me on the icy ground. I leaned into him as he shepherded me and Piper to the steps leading up to the wide porch. Through a window, I spotted a decorated tree and a glowing fire in the hearth. I realized neither of my parents had mentioned Christmas, and even I hadn't brought out our apartment's decorations yet. For years, I had been the only one who cared enough to exhume our phony tree from the storage room. Maybe when I got home I would do the same thing. I had the feeling I would be spending Christmas Eve and Christmas Day alone again.

I glanced over my shoulder and saw the Amish guy helping Betsy, who had no doubt lingered for him. She clutched his arms as they climbed the stairs.

A fierce barking erupted from inside the house as the front door opened with a flourish. A couple in their sixties welcomed me into a spacious foyer with dark wooden floors, throw rugs, and a brass chandelier. A German-shepherd-type dog stood at their side. Piper, being the terrier that she was, bristled but had the good sense to stay in my arms.

"Stomp your feet and come in, everyone," the woman said as she and the man practically pulled me across the threshold.

"Hurry up, slow poke," Brett said, prodding Betsy forward. He plucked her hat off her head and mussed her hair.

"Hey, cut it out." She swung a fist at his shoulder in a mock punch, then smoothed her hair

The air inside felt twenty degrees warmer. In a flash I was stifling. As I unzipped my parka I inhaled the tantalizing aromas of stewing pot roast and baking muffins.

I smiled when Betsy neglected to introduce me. "Hello, Mr. and Mrs. Yoder," I said.

"Please, call us Sam and Marian," the man said, helping me remove my parka. "Around here we go by first names."

Marian, her salt-and-pepper hair parted down the middle and pulled back into a bun, shook my hand. "Delighted to meet you, finally. Betsy has told us so much about you."

I wondered what she'd said.

She must have noticed my worried expression. "Don't fret, dear, nothing bad. We're so glad you were there to help her at work when she first came to town."

"Ah, the classic small-town girl in the big city," Brett said and sniggered.

"This is my obnoxious brother, Brett." Betsy rolled her eyes. "And this is our neighbor, Jesse." Her voice softened to a purr. Oh yeah, she definitely had it bad for this Amish guy.

Jesse raked his fingers through his funky long bangs. "*Ach*, I've lost my hat."

"Hi, Jesse." I tried to make eye contact with him, but he avoided looking at me.

"I'll get you something," Sam told him. "We have plenty of extra hats and beanies." Still carrying my jacket, Sam gestured toward the kitchen. "Let's take the wet clothing into the back room."

Not knowing what to do, I followed them through an expansive kitchen as nice as any I'd ever seen, filled with modern appliances, a substantial refrigerator, and elegant wooden cupboards. The men passed into what appeared to be a utility room, then came back empty-handed.

"Why didn't you park around back?" Sam asked Betsy.

"I'm sorry, Daddy, I'll move the car in the morning." She patted her hair again, clearly conscious of her looks. "It was so windy I didn't know if Diana and I could make it up the back stairs."

"They are steep," Marian said. "Diana, your feet must be freezing. We have extra slippers." I looked at Betsy's feet and noticed she had already found hers. "Betsy, lend her some."

Piper wriggled to get down as the brute of a big dog circled us. "This is Rex," Marian said.

"He's a Malinois, a Belgian shepherd," Brett said, giving the dog a pat. The animal didn't seem to notice, with his attention entirely fixed on Piper, who was shaking.

"Your little dog can't sleep outside tonight," Brett said. "You might as well put her down and let them get to know each other."

"I don't know. She can be feisty." I paused as I envisioned a dog fight, but when I lowered Piper to the floor, the dogs circled each other once, then turned their attention to the stove.

Betsy laughed. "They want food, and so do I. Something smells delish."

"Then get busy and set the table," Marian said. "Jesse, I assume you'll be joining us."

"That would be *gut*, thank you. I should also have asked permission to put my horse in the barn."

"No need." Sam patted him on his back. "You're always welcome. You're like a member of the family."

"Is your wife waiting for you?" I asked with a bit of New York City audacity. I didn't see a wedding band, but maybe the Amish didn't wear them.

"No wife yet," Marian said, smiling. "But soon, right?"

Jesse blushed, but he clamped his lips together.

Rex trotted to the living room door, Piper on his heels. They had apparently decided who was the alpha dog in this pack of two without a skirmish. As they left, a younger woman came in.

"Hi, everyone," she said. Her blond hair was pulled back into a flirty ponytail that swung when she tipped her head. "Hi, Jesse. Some storm, huh?"

"*Yah*, something terrible." He smiled for the first time.

"Diana, this is my little sister, Susie," Betsy said. I knew she'd fill me in later. A rivalry between sisters was sure to be juicy, even if neither could have Jesse. Out of the corner of my eye, I noticed he was, indeed, a hunk, with even features, a strong jaw, and penetrating blue eyes that were finally taking me in, sizing me up. I lifted my chin and returned his gaze.

For a moment we stared at each other, until Betsy broke the tension. "Come on and help me set the table, Diana."

I spun around. Where were my manners? "Sorry, what can I do?"

"How about the flatware?"

Betsy had already spread out a flowered table-cloth and arranged six white plates.

"In that drawer." Betsy pointed to a hutch. "It wouldn't hurt for you to help, too, little sister."

"I'll do the cleaning up after we eat," Susie said. "I promise."

"That seems fair," Marian said. "Including the pots and pans."

Susie groaned. "Okay, but anyone is welcome to help me."

"We'll keep that in mind."

A blast of wind rattled the windows. The falling snow was so dense I could barely see the outline of the barn.

"How will you get home tonight?" I asked Jesse.

"It will be difficult." He looked outside. "I'll sleep in the barn, if Sam and Marian don't mind."

"Now, now, you're welcome to stay here inside with us," Sam said. "I've never seen it snow like this."

"Sure, Jesse, you're always welcome." Marian dumped cooked green beans into a serving dish.

"Will your sisters feed the livestock?" Brett asked Jesse.

"*Yah*, and I'm sure one of their many suitors is already there to help them," Jesse's gaze traveled over to Betsy and then Susie. "And I hired a young man from the area, Melvin, who is very reliable."

Brett crossed his arms, leaned against the counter. "Where were you going tonight, anyway?" He stroked his chin. "Meeting someone?"

Jesse lowered his brows. "I'd rather not say."

Betsy and Susie continued setting the table, but I could tell they were listening, as was I.

"Could I use your phone to call my family?" Jesse asked. "Nancy is in *Rumspringa* and owns a cell phone."

"Of course." Brett dug his phone from his jeans pocket and handed it to Jesse, who tapped in the number.

I wanted to ask how Jesse was allowed to use a cell phone. Apparently, my sweet Amish romance novel hadn't covered all the details.

"Maybe there's someone special you're also wanting to call." Brett tilted his head, and there was something pointed in his gaze. "Though I haven't seen you out with her for a long time."

Jesse ran his hands up his old-fashioned suspenders. "Me? How about you?" I'd heard Amish were known for their humility, but this guy sure wasn't. He reminded me of descriptions of puffed-up roosters. Not that I'd ever seen a live rooster in person.

"Everyone take a seat," Marian said, bringing a pot roast to the table.

I landed between Betsy and Brett, who'd pulled out a chair for me.

"Thanks," I said to him, but he wasn't looking at me. Instead, he grinned at Jesse, who shook his head and lowered himself across the table from Betsy and next to Susie. Sam claimed what must be his usual seat at the end of the table and sliced the roast.

Before I could dig in, the family stopped to pray the longest prayer in the world, or so it seemed. We never prayed before meals at our house.

When I finally started, I ate way too much, and that was before Marian brought out a pecan pie.

"How about a dallop of whipped cream on your pie?" Marian asked. I accepted. And then how could I refuse the second piece when she offered it? I felt my waistband tightening, but I'd be back at our apartment soon, with its empty refrigerator.

I glanced across the room and saw a large and a small bowl of kibble for the dogs. The dogs ate in harmony, with not a single growl.

"This might be the best pecan pie I've ever eaten," I said and meant every word of it.

I looked up and noticed both Brett and Jesse were watching me make a pig of myself, but I didn't care. And if I read their expressions right, they didn't either. I was used to men giving me the eye on the street but didn't expect it out here. Not in Amish country.

Both men glanced away when I smiled at them. Oh well, men were weird everywhere. I thought about Vince and frowned.

A cell phone rang, and all heads popped up. "Hey," Brett said to Jesse, "you're carrying a cell phone?"

"Uh, it's only a couple weeks old," Jesse said. "I thought the ringer was turned off."

"Can't you get yourself into trouble that way?" Betsy asked.

"Not if no one mentions it."

"Are you going to answer the call?" I asked, curiosity burrowing into me.

He didn't. The phone rang two more times, then stopped.

CHAPTER 4

BRETT LEANED ACROSS the table. "What's gotten into you? Are you thinking of jumping the fence?"

What was he asking Jesse? Everyone else at the table seem to be holding their breath. I tried to wait with them, but I was never any good at it.

I turned to Brett. "I don't get it. What fence?"

"He's breaking the *Ordnung*, the Old Order Amish set of unwritten laws."

"Oh?" The word *Ordnung* rang a bell from the novel I'd read. They were strict rules all members of the Amish church must follow, or else they were excommunicated. "Could you get shunned?" I asked Jesse.

"Yes, but it's highly unlikely." Jesse polished off his cup of coffee, seeming unbothered.

Betsy and Susie leaned forward, taking in every word.

Their father said, "Let the poor man finish his dessert."

"Yes," Marian said. "It's none of our business." She offered Jesse more pie, but he shook his head and patted his stomach.

"Thanks for your hospitality, but I need to get to the barn and check my horse."

"As do we," his father said. "Brett, I'm leaving that to you."

"You have horses?" My voice elevated an octave. Betsy hadn't mentioned them. "I love horses." Not that I'd done much riding since summer camp as a preteen.

"Yes, two horses," Sam said. "And they'll need blankets tonight."

"Sorry, Dad," Brett said. "I should have done that when I was out there earlier, but Betsy called me."

"Hey, don't blame your neglect on me," Betsy said.

"*Yah*, I'd better head out to the barn now," Jesse said. "It looks as though the wind has let up."

"I'll go too." Susie shot to her feet.

"Not so fast, young lady," Marian said. "You promised to clean up."

Betsy dabbed the corners of her mouth with her napkin. "I could go with them."

"No." Marian sounded annoyed. "You stay and help your sister."

"How about me?" I asked. "I've always adored horses, and I'd like to see the barn."

Jesse shot me a look of disbelief. "During a blizzard?"

"Sure, come along." Brett stood. "But he's right, you'd better bundle up, and leave your pint-size pup in the house."

Sam chuckled. "Suddenly everyone wants to go outside during a snowstorm? This is a first."

"I need to check on my horse." Jesse headed for the back door.

"And I'm blanketing our horses," Brett said. He turned to me. "Use any boots in the utility room that fit."

"Diana, grab a heavy jacket and a hat too," Betsy said. "We have plenty."

"Wait." Marian moved to a sideboard and pulled a flashlight out of a drawer. "You may need this, Diana." She flicked it on and off.

I took it from her. "Thanks." I couldn't recall the last time I'd used a flashlight.

Brett, Jesse, and I trundled into the utility room, where I stepped into knee-high rubber boots that were a little loose and tall, but who was I to complain? Brett pulled a jacket from the wall and handed it to me.

"This is Betsy's," he said. "I'm sure she won't mind if you wear it."

"And gloves?" Jesse asked him.

"I was getting there." Brett reached into a basket and handed me a pair of leather gloves.

"Thanks." I was relieved I didn't have to wear my favorite suede gloves, purchased last year at Bergdorf Goodman.

Brett shoveled snow off the back steps, then came back inside. "The steps are steep. Better hold onto the railing."

"Okay." I pulled a beanie over my hair and zipped myself into a grungy jacket, nothing I'd ever seen Betsy wear in the city. It was too big for me, but it was better than my city clothes. The gloves were stiff and grimy, so I didn't need to worry about getting them dirty. I turned on my flashlight.

As soon as Brett opened the door, I questioned my wisdom in braving the tempest. A blast of nippy air almost knocked me over. "Are you sure you want to come with us?" Brett asked.

Why was I going outside to begin with? What was I trying to prove? That I was courageous?

"Yes, I want to see the barn." I raised my chin as I stepped out into the darkening world. "It seems as though the storm has let up a little bit." The beautiful brick-red barn loomed in front of me, and the flashlight illuminated the path. Puffy snowflakes floated to the ground. It was quiet, unlike the city I was so used to. I wondered if I'd be able to sleep tonight without blaring horns and sirens in the background.

Brett and Jesse trotted down the stairs. They were chatting in Pennsylvania Dutch again. Were they talking about me? No, I was turning paranoid.

As I stepped forward I felt the heel of my boot skidding away without me. I landed on my rear end with a painful thump and let out a yelp. I should have listened to Jesse and held onto the rail. Well, I had no one to blame but myself.

Both men turned around and clambered back up the stairs. "Are you okay?" Brett asked.

"I'm fine." Was I? Pain radiated across my hip.

"Can you stand?"

"I think so." I felt like crying but wouldn't let them see my agony or embarrassment at being clumsy.

Jesse slid his hand under my elbow. Before I knew it, both men were helping me to my feet, lifting me off the ground.

"Do you want to go back into the house?" Brett asked.

"No, I still want to see the horses." Maybe if I acted fine, I'd feel better. And I really did adore horses.

Both men supported me as I hobbled down the stairs, which were much steeper than I'd expected. Each move sent a painful spasm down my legs, but I continued until we reached the barn's door. Brett pulled it open. I inhaled the musty aroma of livestock and hay I hadn't smelled since I was a kid. I wondered if I could still ride a horse, but tonight wasn't the time to try anything.

Inside, the barn was cavernous and dark. It didn't appear that big on the outside, but now the barn seemed huge. I heard giant wings flapping overhead, followed by a raspy screech. Without a thought I turned and grabbed Brett's sleeve.

"Just a barn owl," he said.

Aiming my flashlight's beam, I looked up and saw a huge, cream-colored bird on a rafter with what must be a rat in its talons. Ugh. I hated rats.

"Owls are better than cats at ridding barns of vermin," Jesse said with a chuckle. He clearly thought I was a sissy, a personality trait New Yorkers refuse to admit to having. Yet my heart beat triple time as I glanced into the rafters.

A horse in a stall near us kicked the wall in an angry fashion. Steam shot from its flared nostrils.

"That's Jesse's feisty stallion," Brett told me. "Don't get too close. He bites."

Jesse's gaze followed mine from the rafters to the stall. "The owl spooked him."

"Why would you keep a horse like that?" I asked.

"Midnight is a retired thoroughbred racehorse," Jesse said. "A fine animal."

"A stallion?" I said. "No wonder he's so ornery."

"How do you know so much?" Jesse asked.

"I used to go to summer camp in Connecticut. I rode a lot there." Those were the happiest days of my life, but now I wondered if my parents just wanted to get rid of me for a month. "The owners kept a stallion for breeding purposes. We were never allowed to go near it."

"Good advice," Brett said. "Come and meet our two horses instead." He led me to the other side of the barn. "Honey is a mare, and Duke a gelding." He brought out several blankets, draped one over Honey and another over Duke. He handed the third to Jesse. "I'll let you do the honors."

"Thanks." Jesse entered Midnight's stall and lay the blanket on the restless animal's back, then cinched it around his belly.

"Is Midnight always like this?" I asked him.

"If I said no, I'd be lying." Jesse closed the stall's gate. "I've had him only a couple of months. He'll settle down. In the meantime, he will pass every-body we meet on the road."

I would never understand the competitive nature of men.

As this thought meandered through my brain, I noticed both of the men were again giving me the look-over out of the corner of their eyes. I returned their gazes until they fell into conversation as if I didn't exist.

CHAPTER 5

"FINALLY, YOU'RE BACK," Betsy said as soon as I opened the door. I wondered if she'd been waiting at the window the whole time I'd been in the barn. "Come in before you freeze."

"I'm fine." Not true. I pulled off the gloves and rubbed my icy fingers together. They barely functioned. I shivered all over.

"You look like you need help." Betsy assisted me as I shed the jacket and hung it on a hook.

The family and I assembled in the kitchen. Sam sat at the head of the table sipping coffee.

"Thanks." I accepted another piece of pie from Marian. This time lemon meringue. "Yummy, my favorite." I worried about my waistline. In New York City, looks were everything.

"Are you sure Jesse won't come in?" Marian asked Brett as she cut a wedge for him.

"He said after the storm blows past, but that could be a while." Brett forked into a yellow piece of ambrosia. "His horse is too agitated. I'd sell that beast, but he won't listen to me."

"I could take Jesse a piece of pie," Betsy said, but her father shook his head.

"I will not have you out there chasing after him."

"But I was just— "

"We've gone all over this." Sam aimed his gaze at Susie. "You too. No chasing after a man who will never be yours. He will soon be married."

"But he owns a cell phone," Betsy said.

"I was surprised to see that." Marian set the pie on the table. "But that doesn't mean he will leave the Amish church."

"Nor has he shown any interest in either of you," Sam said. "Other than being your friend. Be content with that."

Both women lowered their chins. I felt sorry for them, but I couldn't imagine them giving up the internet or TV, let alone driving a car. I know I never would. But I kept quiet for once and savored the melt-in-your-mouth pie. I couldn't remember my mother ever making a pie, or any dessert, now that I thought about it.

"This pie is beyond delicious," I told Marian as I slid the plate into the sink of sudsy water. "Is there anything I can do to help?"

Susie grinned, but Sam said, "And deprive Susie of her commitment to finish cleaning up after dinner? No, thanks." Susie's grin sagged into a scowl.

"Show Diana her room," Marian said to Betsy, who was glancing out the window again toward the barn.

"Uh, okay, follow me, girlfriend."

I lugged my overnight bag up a flight of stairs. Piper shadowed me.

Betsy opened the first door. "Here you go. Right across the hall from the powder room."

"Are you sure it's okay for Piper to sleep up here?" My pooch had already turned in a circle on the hooked rug by the bed and lay down.

"Sure, it's too cold for her to sleep in the car." Betsy offered just the answer I was hoping for. She strolled to the window and looked out toward the barn. "What did you think of our horses?"

I figured her real question was what did I think of Jesse.

"They looked wonderful." I joined her at the window and watched the snowflakes swirl by. I also hoped to see Jesse, if I was honest. "That little mare is more my style."

"Don't want to tackle Jesse's stallion?"

"A girl would be safer jaywalking in rush-hour traffic," I said and meant it. "That, at least, I'm used to. What about you? Would you move back here?"

"I doubt it, unless the right opportunity showed itself."

"And dropped down on one knee?" I leaned against the tall dresser. "Don't try to deny you have a humongous crush on Jesse."

"He and I come from different worlds. Well, we might as well." She pursed her lips together for a moment. "I adore living in Manhattan and all the hustle and bustle, but I can't find the love of my life there."

"Because he lives here?"

"There's no use speculating about what will never happen." Her eyes lost their luster for a second, but Betsy never stayed sad for long. "I have an idea. How about we take my brother and Jesse to the Big Apple when we go back?"

"Would your parents let you do that?"

"Hey, I'm a grown woman." She smoothed the quilt. "I'll just say I want to show my brother my apartment."

"He's never seen it?"

"No, not this one." The corners of her mouth tipped up. "And Jesse has never seen Manhattan, to my knowledge."

"But doesn't he own a farm? Who will take care of it?"

"He'll figure it out. He has Melvin helping him. 'Very reliable,' remember? And nothing much happens in Lancaster County in December."

I sat down on the quilt-covered single bed and listened to its springs creak. "I'd hate to see you disappointed," I said.

She fluffed the pillow. "I could be equally worried for you."

"Huh?"

"Brett," she shot back. "I'd hate to see you disappointed over my brother."

I didn't know how to respond. "Why would you even say that?"

"I saw how you were ogling him. And he kept looking at you." She smirked. "I'd better warn you, as soon as things get serious, he's long gone."

"No worries there," I said. Yes, I thought Brett was attractive, but no way would I move out of the city and up here. And I couldn't imagine him relocating to New York City.

CHAPTER 6

"LET ME KNOW if you need anything,"
Betsy opened the closet door. "There's an
extra bathrobe in here." She covered her mouth to
yawn. "I'll be right next door. Sleep tight."

"Thanks."

She strolled out of the room, closed the door
behind her.

Out of courtesy, I called my parents and listened
to two jovial voices on their respective voice mails
saying they weren't available.

"I'm gone for a couple days," I said to each of
them—first Mom and then Dad. "Out of town with
Betsy. Text me, okay?"

Did they care where I was? I felt like a little lost
waif, always waiting for them to show up. What was
the use of having a daughter if they didn't want

to see her? Maybe I had been a mistake. Maybe Mom had gotten pregnant, and Dad felt obligated to marry her.

Betsy's parents seemed to be perfect, but I knew they probably had problems of their own. Well, no use in comparing or worrying about that now. I just hoped I'd sleep through the night.

I slipped into my pajamas, found magazines on the nightstand, then snuggled between soft sheets and under the gorgeous quilt. It was clearly hand stitched, with bold geometric shapes and colors.

I couldn't imagine there would be anything in an Amish magazine found in Lancaster County that I wanted to read, but as I flipped through the *Connection,* I discovered one interesting article after another of gardening tips. Not that I had a garden in the city.

I perused an article on draft horses plowing a cornfield. I admired each giant animal and the artful way the huge horses matched in both color and size. Gorgeous, and not a tractor in sight.

The weight of my fatigue finally pulled me into the down pillow. I switched off the light by the bed and drifted off to sleep.

I woke later with a start, to the sound of men's voices arguing downstairs. I lay in the tomb of darkness that I knew all too well, listening to a conflict yet again. Piper snuffled under the door and whined.

In a daze, I found my way to the closet and extracted the bathrobe Betsy mentioned, then crept to the door and listened. All I heard was the wind tossing the branches of a nearby tree against the side of the house. I cracked the door and again heard the gruff sound of an angry man.

Sam seemed like a gentle soul. I couldn't imagine him raising his voice, certainly not with a guest in the house. That left Brett and Jesse. But they were like brothers, weren't they?

I moved into the hallway and tiptoed halfway down the stairs before I saw Brett clutching Jesse's shirt collar. Jesse's hand was balled into a fist; he seemed on the verge of throwing a punch. I thought the Amish were nonresistant—not simply pacifists. They wouldn't even defend themselves. That always turn-the-other-cheek way of thinking boggled my mind.

I considered going down and breaking them up if I could. I doubted I was strong enough. Maybe I should go knock on Betsy's door, wake her up, and ask her for help.

I tried to imagine what the two men were arguing about. Me? Nah, neither of them even knew me. I chided myself for being self-centered.

I crawled back to bed and pulled up the covers, but I couldn't sleep. I tossed and turned as I listened to the unfamiliar sounds of the wind rattling the storm windows.

I finally dozed off into a sea of tranquility. In what seemed like a few hours later, my eyes cracked open. I saw light slanting through the window. The savory aromas of coffee, eggs, and bacon crept up the stairs and under the door. Piper stretched to her feet and sniffed the air. When I tugged on the bathrobe and opened the door my pooch zipped past me and scampered down the stairs.

I took a quick shower and decided my hair would have to dry on its own. I didn't want to keep the others waiting for their breakfast. I dug through my bag and extracted a white turtleneck, a baby-blue fleece vest and jeans, and found my borrowed slippers. I glanced in the mirror to make sure I was presentable without makeup, then descended the stairs.

"Good morning, Diana. How did you sleep?" Marian asked. "Tea, coffee, or hot chocolate?"

I couldn't help myself. I compared her to my mother, who always slept in. Had she ever made coffee for my father or me?

"If your coffee tastes half as good as it smells, I'd be a fool to pass it up."

She smiled as she poured dark liquid into a mug.

"Sugar? Cream? This coffee is dark." She was right. My mouth puckered as I took my first sip. I dribbled a generous splash of cream into it and stirred it with a spoon, watched it swirl into the coffee. I tried a second sip and found it to my liking.

Sam ambled in through the back door, where he traded his boots for fur-lined slippers. "I see our guest has arisen, but not our children." He poured himself an ample amount of coffee and drank it black.

"Not even Jesse?" I asked, then wished I hadn't.

Sam's eyebrows jumped a skosh. "You hear all that ruckus a couple hours ago?"

"No, but last night . . ." I pressed my lips together. It was none of my business. I looked out the window and saw a frozen white world that reminded me of the old movie *Dr. Zhivago*.

"Jesse went out to check his horse early this morning. It bolted out of the barn." Sam shook his head. "Jesse chased after him."

"My best guess is the horse went back to its own barn, not that far away," Marian said. "Horses do that."

"In all the snow?" My hunch was I would never see Jesse again. Which shouldn't matter but I felt a vague sadness deep in my heart.

"Did someone say something about horses?" Brett wandered into the room freshly showered and shaven. His damp hair was tousled.

"How about some eggs, everyone?" Marian said. "I've got bacon."

"Sounds good, Mom. Thank you." He sat at the table and motioned for me to sit next to him.

Sam told Brett what happened to Midnight. Brett's expression didn't change.

"That horse could be on the other side of the county by now, or trapped in the snow."

"Oh, I hope not." Marian's hand wrapped her throat. "Couldn't you go out in the truck and help him?"

"I suppose, if he wants my help."

"Why wouldn't he? Is there something you're not telling us?" Marian hesitated, then brought a platter of scrambled eggs and bacon to the table. "Please serve yourself, Diana." She handed me a large spoon.

Brett eyed the eggs and waited for me to serve myself. As I did, he picked up a piece of bacon and chomped into it. Marian brought English muffins and freshly cooked biscuits to the table. I selected a biscuit and relished its warmth. Steam escaped as I broke it open, then smeared it with butter and strawberry jam.

"Here, girl." Marian led Piper to the dog food bowls, where Rex was already gobbling kibble. She showed Piper the smaller bowl of dog food.

"You're not going to go over and help your best friend?" Sam asked Brett.

"Who said he was my best friend?"

"Since when this change in attitude?" Marian asked.

Brett slathered butter on an open biscuit.

Marian's eyes told me she was worried. "Can you call Jesse on his new phone?"

Brett frowned. "I don't have the number." He forked into his eggs and swallowed a mouthful, followed by a swig of coffee. "Delicious as usual, Mom."

I tried not to stare at him. Not many men could compete with his good looks, but his attitude irked me. Brett ignored me and continued to enjoy his meal. So did I, but I felt tension in this room.

Sam tried again. "What gives, son? I thought you two were close friends."

"Yeah, well, I thought he was a straight arrow, not a liar."

"What do you mean?" Marian asked. "Is this about the phone?"

Brett shook his head. "Weren't you planning to go to his wedding next month?" Brett asked.

"Next month?" I sounded like a squawking parrot. My hand raised to cover my mouth. Marian had teased Jesse about getting married soon, but I didn't realize there was actually a wedding planned. Or a specific bride. Not that I should care.

"Yes." Sam stroked his chin. "I suppose that could be postponed because of the snow."

Brett snorted. "No, it's permanently postponed because Jesse changed his mind."

Sam and Marian sat with that bombshell for a minute.

"Naomi must be heartbroken," Marian said finally. "But better to find out before the wedding, don't you think?"

"Here's what burns me up." Brett's voice turned harsh. "Jesse told me last night he only just confessed to her he's calling it off."

"That's why he was out in the storm?" Marian asked.

"Yes. And all the wedding preparations are still in motion."

My jaw dropped. Jesse was as bad as Vince. I remembered my feelings of desperation and fury when I found out he was engaged to another woman so quickly after our breakup. Those feelings still weighed on my shoulders like blocks of cement.

"But that doesn't explain how his horse ran off," Sam said.

"If you ask me, he let it escape so that he could get away for the day." Brett crossed his arms. "Jesse's always had a wild streak, but I thought he'd settled down."

"What are you all talking about?" Betsy glided into the room. "Something to do with Jesse?"

"His horse ran away," Sam said. "He went looking for it."

"Let's go over to his farm and see if he found him." Betsy snagged a biscuit.

Brett was still shaking his head. "I'm not going anywhere in this weather."

"Then I will," Betsy said. "How about it, Diana?"

"Hold on, daughter." Sam maneuvered himself toward the doorway, blocking Betsy's exit. "Did you know Jesse is all set to get married next month?"

Betsy blinked, looking shocked. "Why didn't you tell me?"

I attempted to be invisible as Marian motioned for her to have a seat at the table. "Well, we were trying to save your feelings. We knew . . ." she trailed off.

"You knew what?"

Sam joined them at the table. "Your mother and I were trying to do what we thought was best."

Betsy was clearly hurt. "What you thought was best? That's why I moved to New York—to get away from your meddling."

Marian moved to Sam's side and glanced at me. "Let's not allow this to become a family squabble when we have company." She waited until Betsy looked at her. "We knew you have a soft spot for Jesse, that's all."

"To put it mildly." Brett still sounded angry. "She's practically thrown herself at him for years."

"I have not." Betsy stomped her foot and turned to her mother. "Are you sure he's getting married?"

"I'm not sure of anything, but a wedding is—or was—planned."

Betsy's features drooped as she turned to me and said, "Amish weddings in Lancaster County are huge affairs that take months of planning in preparation. And celery. Lots and lots of celery." She paused, then turned back to her parents. "Who's the girl?"

"You must know her," Brett said. "Naomi Stoltzfus. She grew up here."

"Long red hair?" she asked. Brett nodded. Betsy stood and appeared to be putting on a brave face. "So what's the problem? This snow will melt, and the happy couple can be on their way."

Everyone paused. "I hate to give you false hope," Brett finally said, "but I think Jesse had a change of heart." He selected a muffin and layered on butter and jam. "The way he's been acting for the last couple days, I have no idea what to expect. I pity the woman who tried to get him to commit." He looked at Betsy. "Including you."

CHAPTER 7

THIRTY MINUTES LATER I sat behind Brett in the back seat of his red four-wheel-drive Ford extended cab pickup. Betsy perched in the front passenger seat as we motored up the lane, then took an immediate U-turn and rolled down a different road. Jesse's sprawling farm was impressive, the crisp white paint echoing the snow.

Brett pulled the truck into the yard between the house and an enormous barn. He skidded to a halt. I figured he was in a grouchy mood by his jerky actions. As I got out of the pickup behind Betsy, the snow felt slippery beneath my boots. This time I would not land on my rear.

Jesse poked his head out the barn door but didn't wave. With cautious steps, he proceeded toward us.

"What brings you by?" Jesse asked.

"You know." Brett glared at him.

"You've come to force me to marry against my will?"

"Why didn't you say something about getting married?" Betsy asked. "No one said a word at dinner last night." She didn't seem angry at Jesse. Quite the contrary, I thought she looked hopeful.

"He was taking the coward's way out." Brett jammed his hands into his jacket pockets.

Jesse didn't respond. Instead, his deep blue eyes locked onto mine. I felt like a dummy for being attracted to him, but he really was cute. He was also obviously not trustworthy nor in search of a mate. He already had one.

Brett wasn't finished. "I can't believe you're treating Naomi this way. Do her parents know?"

"I'll take no lectures from you," Jesse snapped back.

Though I'd never met her, I felt sorry for Naomi. I knew all too well what it was like to be dumped like stale tuna, or whatever the Amish ate. "We came to ask about your horse," I said to Jesse. "Did you get Midnight back?"

"Eventually." Jesse glanced toward the barn. "He got caught up in some brambles. I had to bandage one leg."

"May I see him?" I didn't want to miss my chance. Tomorrow Betsy and I would head back to the city, assuming the roads were cleared.

"*Yah*, he's quite a bit calmer today." Jesse smiled at me.

"That's good news." Brett's words were laced with sarcasm. "We wouldn't want you to get kicked in the head."

How could their friendship take a radical turn in such a short amount of time?

We followed Jesse into his colossal barn. Betsy hurried to match his long strides. "What are you going to do?" she asked. "Will Naomi's father come and fetch you when he finds out?"

Jesse shrugged. "He's an ornery buzzard, and a bishop, but he'll probably sic his deacon on me first to give me a good scolding. See if I come around."

I admired the gorgeous black stallion but kept my distance. "Can they force you into marrying if you don't want to?" I asked him.

"Her father can turn the whole district against me, and no doubt will." Jesse looked and sounded serious.

"I have an idea." Betsy bounced on the balls of her feet. "Yesterday Diana and I were thinking about asking Brett if he wanted to go back to the city with us tomorrow. Jesse, we could take you too. Give you a break."

"Sounds like the coward's way out," Brett said. "Jesse should stay here and face the music."

"But if he doesn't love her . . ." Betsy's words trailed off.

"He made a commitment, something Jesse's never been good at keeping."

Betsy got in her brother's face. "How can you say that? He took over this farm when his father couldn't work anymore."

"Big deal." Brett stared down into her face. "A free farm. Acres and acres of the finest land in the county. Who would turn that down?"

Jesse looked mad enough to throw a fist into Brett's jaw, but he contained himself. "I'm sorry, Brett. I know it's my own fault, but I feel trapped."

"Then why did you ask her to marry you?" I heard myself say, though it was none of my business. Yes, it was. Betsy was my dear friend.

"Not out of love, and I doubt she loves me."

"Don't sell yourself short," Betsy said.

He gave a small shrug. "I pity her for the grief her parents will no doubt put her through. I also know the man who she wants to marry. But her parents refused to let them date."

"Seriously?" Brett lessened the distance between him and Jesse.

"I wouldn't lie to you, Brett."

"I'm not so sure about that." Brett folded his arms across his brawny chest.

Jesse ignored the taunt and strolled over to his stallion's stall. The horse's attention riveted to Jesse, its ears moved forward. "Come on, fella." Jesse smoothed Midnight's powerful neck, then scratched the elegant animal between the ears.

Midnight nickered softly in response. His lower jaw loosened in an easy-going manner. Even his tail swished back and forth. Yes, this was Jesse's, and only Jesse's, horse.

"Sure, I'll go to the Big Apple with you," Brett said. "Sounds like fun. It's been years."

"And how about you?" Betsy asked Jesse.

"Yah. In fact, I'd go today. But where will we sleep?"

"My parents' apartment." I spun the scenario over in my mind. They'd always told me I could bring friends over anytime I wanted. But did they really mean two grown men from Lancaster County? Still, I said, "The apartment is huge and has extra bedrooms. My friends are always welcome."

"We could have a blast in NYC," Betsy said.

"It sounds *wunderbaar*," Jesse said. "I need to check it over with my sisters and Melvin first, though. Come into the house."

"Wait, I don't feel right about helping Jesse skip town," Brett said.

Jesse rolled his eyes. "Will you at least come in and say hello to my sisters?"

We followed in his wake, crunching through the snow toward the imposing home. I had to admit, I was surprised at how fashionable it all looked. A wraparound porch supported a swing and chairs that would be delightful in the summer. No wonder an Amish woman wanted to marry Jesse. He must be the most eligible Amish bachelor in Lancaster County.

The door swung open. Two young women, probably in their early twenties, welcomed us. "Please come in," said the taller of the two. "I'm Nancy, and this is my younger sister, Cathy." Both were sandy-haired, from what I could see peeking out from under their bonnets, and attractive without a bit of makeup. They wore the traditional apron, dress, and heart-shaped head coverings I'd read about in my Amish novel. I peeked to see if their aprons were fastened with long straight pins. Yes. Those pins looked lethal.

We stomped the snow off our feet and left our boots in the back utility room next to an old-fashioned wringer washer. I felt as though I'd plummeted back into another century. I couldn't imagine myself doing laundry like this, but then again, I'd heard that line drying left sheets enveloped with a sweet aroma.

Nancy led us into the kitchen, where I was met with the fragrance of cooking apples and dough. The girls noticed my gaze traveling across their attire and they tittered.

Jesse lassoed their attention. The family spoke for a few minutes in Pennsylvania Dutch. I assumed he was telling them he was going to be out of town for a few days. They seemed worried, but nodded.

Jesse turned to Brett. "It's all settled. I could take off today—"

"Not so fast, buddy." Brett lowered his brows. "You'd better stick around to see if the bishop is going to pay you a call."

Jesse winced. "Usually he does not perform such duties himself."

"But Naomi is his daughter," Nancy said.

Brett looked surprised. "Do your sisters know what's going on?"

"Yah, I think everyone in the county does. Gossip flies around like a flock of starlings."

"Naomi must be devastated."

"No, I don't think so." Jesse worried his lips. "If anything, she is relieved."

His story didn't add up.

"I can't imagine a woman would agree to marry a man she didn't love," I said, as if I were an expert.

"Some marry for money," Betsy answered. "I'll bet it happens even among the Amish."

"Jesse's not so bad to look at either, if you like that type." Wait, had I said that out loud?

Everyone gawked at me. I felt blood radiating up my neck and into my cheeks. His sisters both giggled. Brett and Betsy looked unamused.

Like choreographed swimmers, Jesse's sisters served coffee, then brought out plates and arranged them on the table. Brett pulled out a chair for me. We sat at the table as the girls passed around a platter of freshly baked cookies.

I scanned the room and noticed there was no Christmas decor, other than a few sprigs of holly. Not even a tree and obviously no colorful electric lights.

Our snack was interrupted when a car pulled up the driveway. I heard several doors slam. Jesse shot to his feet and looked out the window overlooking the barnyard. He let out a puff of air.

"Naomi's father?" Brett asked in a way that told me he was enjoying the situation. He chuckled. "Inevitable."

CHAPTER 8

JESSE SHOT HIM a glare. His sisters hastened to the window, then Nancy murmured,
"Deacon Thomas and Bishop Harold."

"A bishop?" I asked. "From the Catholic church?"

"No," Brett said, "from the Amish church."

"They're church leaders, chosen by lot," Betsy
explained.

Brett saw my confusion. "When men are baptized, they agree to serve the community if chosen.
Being a bishop is a full-time, nonpaying, lifetime
job. We've known men and their families who
cried when their names were drawn." He glanced
at the window. "Bishop Harold welds a lot of power
among the Amish."

"But they're riding in a car," I said.

"Probably hired a driver."

We were interrupted by the sound of heavy foot-steps mounting the back stairway, followed by crisp rapping on the door.

"Well?" Brett asked Jesse. "Are you going to open it?"

"Go get the door," Jesse told Cathy, but she stared back at him.

Brett shook his head. "You get the door, Jesse. This is your problem, not hers."

Jesse stood and moved to the back door. I heard a man's low, gravelly voice speaking Pennsylvania Dutch, then the stomping of boots that caused the whole house to shudder.

A man dressed in black removed his brimmed hat as he entered the room, but held onto it. He clearly wasn't planning to stay. He was not large in stature, I noticed, but his bushy beard and shaved upper lip gave him an intimidating heft. Behind him came another solemn-looking fellow. He was younger, with the same funky hairdo as Jesse, graying at the temples. He wasn't half as cute.

"This is Bishop Harold and Deacon Thomas," Jesse said, mostly to me. Everyone else seemed to know each other. He turned to his new guests. "Coffee?"

Both men shook their heads. "This is not a social call," said the older man, "Although it does appear you have guests and are enjoying yourself while my Naomi is at home crying."

Jesse looked the bishop straight in the eye but said nothing.

"Here I am, soon to be a grandfather," the bishop said, "but I have no son-in-law."

What? Naomi was pregnant? Brett and Betsy both wore dumbfounded expressions. My respect for Jesse plummeted. But then, I saw that even Jesse looked surprised.

"If she told you I'm the father of the child she carries, she's lying."

The room was still for a minute before Jesse continued with conviction. "I don't know what Naomi told you, but she and I never . . ." His hand swiped his mouth.

"Why should I believe you over my own daughter?" Harold tugged on his ample beard. His eyes looked kind; I knew he was a good man in a tough position. "I never should have allowed her to date you," he said. "You were not my choice."

"I wish you hadn't," Jesse said. "Naomi is in love with someone else. We all know it."

The bishop's hand moved to his mouth as if containing a barrage of angry words. I felt sorry for his terrible predicament. Any father would feel protective of his daughter under such circumstances.

"You should speak to Naomi about this," Jesse said.

"How dare you tell me what to do?" Harold's voice was full of wrath, erupting from his ample belly. He took a deep breath almost immediately, probably seeking that Amish nonresistance. His gaze turned to me for the first time.

"This is Brett's sister's friend from New York City," Jesse said.

I raised a hand. "Hi, I'm Diana." I felt like scurrying under the table, away from the conflict, but gathered my courage instead and stood to pour a cup of coffee. I held it out to the bishop. Much to my surprise, his hand reached out to take it.

Cathy poured the deacon a cup too. "Please have a seat." They both hesitated, then turned to hang their hats on wall pegs. They sat on the edges of their chairs, but the negative energy was lessened. Nancy brought a platter of cinnamon rolls to the table.

A long block of silence ensued.

"We didn't come here for sustenance." The bishop's gaze zeroed in on a cinnamon roll.

I wondered if it was bad manners to take one for myself, but I couldn't resist. "May I?"

"Yah," Cathy and Nancy answered in unison. They produced clean dessert plates and paper napkins. Everyone reached for the platter except the bishop and Jesse, who still stood leaning against the counter. I wondered what Jesse was trying to do, as the bishop was angry enough without being further goaded.

Knuckles knocked on the glass panes of the back door.

Cathy flitted to the door, allowing a flock of chattering young Amish women into the kitchen. When they saw Harold and Thomas, their eyes widened, and they stopped short, bumping into each other like cartoon characters.

"*Ach*," one of the girls said.

"A quilting frolic," Cathy said to Jesse, who was glaring at her. "I thought I told you."

Jesse stood tall. "No, you never mentioned a thing, or I would have said no."

"But we need to finish Naomi's wedding quilt," Nancy said.

"I told you this morning not to finish it," Jesse said his voice gruff.

I was thoroughly miffed at Jesse by this point but managed to keep my thoughts to myself for a change.

"Their driver already left, and it's almost done," Nancy said, not backing down.

"And it's too pretty not to finish." Cathy turned to the young women. "Take off your coats. Come on in."

Betsy's gaze glommed onto me. "Maybe Diana would like to help," she suggested.

I didn't know how to quilt. "I'd only be a hinderance."

"Then you must learn," the bishop said. "Finishing my daughter's wedding quilt is a wonderful idea." He pivoted toward the girls. "You may be excused. Off you go."

Their spirits elevated, they sped toward the core of the house, all jabbering at once. I was tempted to follow their joyous sounds, but I didn't speak the language or know how to assist them.

He glanced at me. "You don't wish to help?"

"Sorry," I said, "I don't know how to quilt."

Betsy saved me from further embarrassment. "She's our guest and won't be in town long enough to learn how."

"Then we won't keep you." The bishop tugged on his voluminous beard and dismissed us with a wave.

"Hey, this is my house," Jesse said, "and they are my guests."

The bishop's upper lip lifted. "Did your parents never teach you good manners?"

"Maybe we should take off," Betsy said. Her voice rose at the end like she was asking a question.

"Only if I can come with you," Jesse said. "Let me pack my bag."

"You'd run away?" Bishop Harold said. He pressed his lips together into a straight, hard line. The deacon shook his head, his scraggly beard not covering his disgust.

Jesse ignored them.

Brett glanced outside at the cotton puffs of snow that were sailing down again. "I'm not driving anywhere farther than my own house today. Those roads will be slick as—well, slick."

"But we have to go tomorrow," Betsy said. "Or else Diana and I might get fired."

I considered the possibility. I'd never been fired before. Would Mr. Simonton's face turn beet red as he marched me out the door? Would my coworkers, other than kind-hearted Betsy, snigger? Probably.

A short rap at the back door snagged our attention. A clean-shaven, middle-aged man in modern dress let himself in and spoke to the bishop. "I'm freezing out there, and I'd better make my way to my next stop before I'm stuck in Jesse's barnyard for the night."

"I'm so sorry," the bishop said, standing. "I forgot the time."

"Do you want me to leave you here?" the man asked. "I might be able to stop by later, but I can't guarantee it, the way this snow is building up."

The bishop glanced at Jesse.

"It looks as if our conversation will have to come to an end for now. As soon as the snow lets up, I will be back." The bishop turned to the driver. "All right. I'd better come with you now. I don't wish to get stuck here."

I could see Jesse shivering, pretending to be afraid. How immature. The bishop did not appreciate his clowning around, either, but merely planted his black wool hat on his head, buttoned his coat, and followed the driver out toward the back door without saying goodbye.

"Nice to meet you," I called after him. At least one of us was going to be polite. But he didn't respond.

CHAPTER 9

"GOOD RIDDANCE," JESSE said as we
listened to the departing vehicle's tires
spin and leave the barnyard. "Finally, I can relax
in my own home."

"Like all your problems just disappeared with
him?" Brett asked.

"Not all of them, but maybe with Harold gone .
. ." He shrugged.

Brett shook his head. "If she's with child . . ."

"If she is," Jesse stressed. "Like I said, the *poppi*
isn't mine."

"Have you no feelings for Naomi?" I asked.

"Sure, we've been friends since childhood."
Jesse stopped and winced as wind slapped a branch
against the side of the house. "*Ach*, more snow."

"Don't try to change the subject." Brett tilted his head. "As I recall, you and Naomi were always sweet on each other."

"That seems a lifetime ago. And like I said, she's smitten, head over heels, with . . . never mind, I promised not to tell anyone."

"But do you love her?" Betsy asked, her voice tentative.

Brett looked over to her and frowned. "Why don't you take Diana into the other room? We should not subject our guest to this."

Her shoulders slumped, but she nodded. "Want to?" she asked me in a lackluster voice.

Phooey, I was going to miss out on their conversation.

"Lead the way." I followed Betsy toward the sounds of chattering and mirth.

We found the young women gathered around a quilt spread out on a wooden frame like a table. When they saw me, they fell silent.

"Please speak in English," Betsy said. "This is my friend Diana, from New York City."

They all dipped their chins shyly, but eventually a couple said, "Hello" and "Nice to meet you."

"She won't bite," Betsy said.

They giggled, then bent their heads and continued sewing. I tried not to stare, but their simple look, without makeup or jewelry, was so foreign to me. Yet I could see that each young woman radiated warmth.

"Want to give it a try?" Betsy asked me. I scanned the quilt and saw they'd finished sewing the fabric pieces together and were now hand-quilting the layers to each other with the greatest of precision—tiny, little stitches, all even.

"Uh, I'd better let them do it." I could picture myself messing up or pricking my finger with a needle and bleeding on the eggshell-white fabric. I had never felt so inadequate.

"Another time, I'll give you a quilting lesson on a simple pattern," Betsy said. "We have plenty of scraps at home."

"Use a log cabin pattern," a young woman said in a high-pitched voice. "That's the best one to start with."

Acts of generosity, I knew, but I still felt ill at ease. "Okay, I guess." I turned to Betsy and whispered, "I'd rather hear what Jesse and your brother are talking about."

She whispered in my ear, "Me too. It's not as though Brett doesn't have secrets of his own."

Curiosity spiked into me. "Such as . . ."

Her face went pale. "I shouldn't tell."

I'd have to wait to get her alone. "What could be so terrible? He robbed a bank or something?"

"Shush."

The girls fell silent. I realized I was speaking too loudly.

Brett poked his head in the room. "I'm going to check on the pond. Jesse wants to go ice-skating, of all things."

Well, at least it sounded as if their dispute had been resolved. "We could all ice-skate in Central Park when we go to the city," I said, "or at Rockefeller Center and see the Christmas tree."

"Sounds fantastic," Betsy said, glancing out the window. "Maybe we should practice today. I'll bet Jesse's sisters have ice skates we could borrow. There were eight kids total, so there should be plenty."

"Eight? Seriously?" As an only child, I couldn't imagine it. I'd spent too many lonely days in the silence of our apartment. There was so much about the Amish that didn't make sense. I could never live like that, for sure. Or could I, now that I thought about the comfort and support of a large family.

I felt sorry for Naomi, whoever she was. If she was pregnant, it would be hard to hide in a community like this, even under a loose dress and apron. Women needed to stick together. Did that include Vince's new wife, though? I thought of my ex and wondered how he was doing with married life. I knew I shouldn't spend another moment thinking about him. He was a cheater.

"Come on while the snow has let up." Betsy interrupted my thoughts. "So what if we're not in the Big Apple. We'll skate here." She laughed, and I realized that I didn't want to rush back to the city either.

CHAPTER 10

I STOOD IN AWE as Jesse skimmed across the frozen pond behind his barn. He didn't seem to notice me. No doubt his mind was teaming with a multitude of thoughts.

He slowed, then his torso started to spin like a ballet dancer—so fast I couldn't make out his features. Just as quickly as he started, he stopped, only a couple of feet away from me.

"Wow." I tried to gather my composure.

He wore a black wool jacket, a beanie, and a grin. "Be sure to tie your laces before you skate," he told me.

"I was about to." The skates looked decades old, but I didn't want to come off as negative and spoiled. I was fortunate to have them.

He shrugged. "If you say so." He was mocking me, but at least we were speaking. His steely-blue eyes captured me like a bird in a net. For a second, I couldn't escape. I shook off the feeling and sat on a bench at the side of the pond, focusing on tightening and then tying the laces.

When I was done, Jesse took my hands and pulled me to my feet. My ankles wobbled like Jell-O.

"Wait, I'll help you." From out of nowhere, Brett stood at my side. His hand reached out and slid under my elbow, steadying me.

Jesse glared at Brett, then glided away across the pond.

"I haven't skated for years," I told Brett. I recalled the many afternoons I went ice-skating as a child. I'd been graceful and capable back then. Well, those days were long gone. Now I felt like a klutz.

His hand under my elbow, Brett guided me around the frozen pond. When I finally felt confident enough to look up, I was wowed to see the back of the barn, cloaked in white and guarded by trees standing like arctic sentinels. The words to "Winter Wonderland" described this place.

"Are you okay?" Brett asked me.

I cracked a smile. "I thought skating was like riding a bike: you never forgot. But clearly I have."

"Bet you'll get the hang of it." His attempt to bolster my confidence wasn't working.

Betsy skated past us, wearing a Cheshire Cat smile. "You two having fun?"

"Your brother is keeping me from toppling over."

Betsy nodded and skated toward Jesse.

"She should keep her distance from him," Brett said and started to follow her.

"Hey, don't go too far away," I called. I was still upright, but my ears felt cold, and I knew I looked clumsy.

He spoke over his shoulder. "You're doing fine."

I wasn't, but I tried to manage by myself. I was the girl who could do anything on her own, after all. I'd practically raised myself, compared to the closeness of the families I saw here. I'd ridden the subway or taken a cab to school and was never surprised when my parents didn't show up for dinner or school functions. They even missed my graduation. I'd wager neither knew that I'd majored in psychology and minored in art history in college.

I realized I'd sped up as I let my thoughts drift. Now I was going too fast, out of control. My feet were moving faster than my body, but I couldn't slow down. I careened right into the group on the other side of the pond, slamming into Jesse.

"Oops," I said. "Sorry."

His arm slid around my shoulder to hold me upright. "Not a problem."

Betsy glided to my other side and slid her arm through the bend of my elbow. "I'll be your skating buddy," she said. "Unless you want to make it a trio," she asked Jesse.

For a few minutes, the three of us skated along together, with me in the middle and our legs moving in tandem. Then Jesse spun away. My, what a moody man he was.

I glanced up at the house to see the Amish quilters watching us, their faces pressed against the windowpanes. Was that why he'd pulled away, to avoid more gossip about his antics?

In ways, I felt sorry for Amish women, living with so little freedom. But in other ways, I felt very close to them. Vince jilted me exactly like Jesse was abandoning Naomi. I wondered if I would ever date again, which made me think about Jesse and Brett. Would I have either one, even if they were interested? I could never be happy living here out in the sticks. Even Betsy had moved away. Yet I found myself looking at the women in the window, all so close together. And Betsy and Brett's parents were wonderful.

The icy air bit into my face, and the snow started to fall again.

Betsy skated next to me but spoke loud enough for the men to hear. "Does hot chocolate sound good?"

"Yes," I said. "Anything chocolate always sounds good."

"Come on into the house," Jesse said. "My sisters will fix you some."

"Or I can do it." Betsy led me to the bench at the edge of the pond. "I know how." What was she up to? Trying to impress Jesse, no doubt.

"Maybe skating at Rockefeller Center or in Central Park will be more fun," I said.

"Eventually," Betsy agreed. "I hope we can go back tomorrow. I don't feel comfortable driving on the roads when they're this icy. Maybe I'll get Brett to drive."

"Do you think he would?" I felt warmer just thinking about him in the car with us. Okay, maybe I had a wee bit of a crush on him too. Or something.

"Brett and you would make the cutest couple," Betsy whispered out of nowhere.

"Suddenly you're a matchmaker?"

"Well, why not? You two could get married. You and I would be sisters. Sisters-in law, but wouldn't that be fun?"

I'd always wanted a sister. "He'd leave Lancaster County, just like that?"

"No guarantees, but I did."

"Would you ever move back if the circumstances were right?"

"You mean if Jesse asked me to stay?" She lowered her voice. "Probably, but that's not going to happen. He officially joined the Amish church last year. I doubt the bishop would let me get baptized." She scanned the area. "Anyway I like my phone and driving too much."

"Does Jesse drive a car?"

"He stashed an old junker behind one of those outbuildings." She tipped her head toward a structure I assumed housed farm equipment. "But before he gets married, I expect he'll have to get rid of it, just like his phone."

We were interrupted by Brett, who called to us. "I'm taking off. Anyone want to come with me?"

"I do, give me a minute." I carried my skates up to Jesse's utility room, with Betsy plodding after me.

"Hey, brother dearest, you can't just leave me here, so I guess I'm coming too."

"I was thinking of going out to a restaurant for a late lunch," Brett said. "Hot chocolate and cookies isn't enough to keep me filled."

"You're hungry already?" Betsy said, sarcasm warping her voice.

"Yeah, I worked up an appetite. Anyone want to go with me?"

"Sounds fun," Jesse said. "I want to come."

"As you like. We're going to Dieners."

Jesse's face contorted. "No, not there."

"Afraid you'll run into anyone special?"

"It's a very popular eating spot for the Amish," Betsy explained to me. "English too."

"I feel weird being called English." I trudged along next to her through the snow.

"Even I'm considered an Englisher to the Amish," she said.

We reached Brett's pickup. Betsy followed Jesse into the cab's back seat.

"Want to stop by Naomi's?" Brett asked Jesse.

"If that's your game, let me out right now." Jesse reached for the door handle just as Brett turned on the engine.

"Settle down. I'm not out to embarrass her like that." Brett gunned the engine; the truck fishtailed out of the lane.

Sunshine peeked from behind the clouds, causing the snow on the ground to sparkle like a zillion faceted jewels. I was grateful that trees laden with snow hadn't toppled over and blocked the road. As that thought cruised through my mind, I heard a branch crash to the ground in the field alongside the barn. The spectacle made me jump. I was used to all kinds of dangers in the city, but not like this. I felt comfortable surrounded by skyscrapers and posh hotels, with the subway in easy reach if it started snowing.

CHAPTER 11

BRETT FOLLOWED A snow plow and was content to drive at its speed for half an hour. As we gained elevation, Jesse spoke. "Where are you taking us?" Looking worried, Jesse clasped one of Brett's shoulders from behind. "Turn around and take me home."

Brett chuckled. "No worries. We're going to an English restaurant. No one will recognize you." He took a left and steered his vehicle into a parking lot.

I read the sign aloud. "New Holland Inn."

"This place is fancy, Brett," Betsy said. "Are you sure we're dressed up enough?"

"Yes." He cut the engine. "We're here for lunch not prom night." He directed us into the hotel and to the restaurant.

Minutes later, a solemn-faced hostess lead us toward a table with white linen cloth napkins, tucked into a corner.

"Trying to hide us?" Brett asked her. His tone bordered on belligerent. "We want to sit by the tree. How about it?"

"As you wish." The woman moved us over to a table in the center of the room, beside a Christmas tree decked in gold and silver.

"This is more like it," he said, as she pulled out chairs for us. I scanned the room and saw three other tables filled with diners, who looked like well-to-do tourists—all staring at us. Well, I was used to ignoring gawking tourists in Manhattan.

"I'll pick up the tab," Brett said to the waitress.

Betsy grinned. "If you insist, brother dearest."

Jesse removed his hat and raked his hand through his hair. "I don't feel comfortable in here. Why didn't you tell me to dress differently?"

"You look fine," Betsy said from the chair next to his. "No one is very dressed up. Look at me." She wore jeans and a turquoise-blue turtleneck. Her hair was pulled back into a ponytail.

"But it's not the same. Everyone can tell I'm Amish."

"We passed a barbershop about a block back," Brett said. "You could trot down there and get your hair cropped. Or I think they have a beauty salon right here in the building."

"Why are you ridiculing me?" Jesse gave Brett the evil eye.

"Because I figure you want to look good in front of Diana," Brett shot back.

I pretended not to hear them, covering my embarrassment by grabbing my napkin and flattening it across my lap.

"No squabbling, fellas," Betsy said. "What's gotten into you two?"

An older couple walking past our table slowed to stare at Jesse, the only Amish person here. But hadn't all these people come to Lancaster County to see men like him?

A waiter produced a basket laden with rolls, muffins, breadsticks, and a ramekin of creamy butter. Jesse seemed more confident as he slathered butter onto his bread and chomped into it. "Very good."

Betsy giggled. "When we get to New York City, I can show you our favorite restaurants."

"Why don't you ever take me?" Brett asked her.

"Because you never visit," she shot back.

We kept up the lighthearted conversation throughout our meal, but I noticed Jesse kept glancing out the window and at the entranceway. Clearly, he was nervous in here. I wondered how he would feel in Manhattan but reassured myself that with the myriad of people from all over the world, he would be fine. He'd blend right in.

Betsy started planning our return to New York the next day. "Do you think the roads are clear enough? I need to get the car back to Annie." She turned to Jesse. "Still want to come with us?"

He nodded with enthusiasm. "I want to go. This might be my last chance at freedom. My only opportunity to leave."

"Okay," Brett finally said, "As long as we stop off at Naomi's house today. I want to make sure you're not sneaking away without telling her."

Betsy sagged but said, "That sounds reasonable." Without allies, Jesse conceded.

Forty minutes later, with the world cloaked in velvety white, Brett steered his pickup down a twisting lane heavy with snow. He glanced over and saw me grasping on to the armrest. "Don't worry, my Ford has four-wheel drive."

"Good to know." Manhattan was flat, with most of the streets at right angles, but these hills and sharp curves were hard to get used to.

Bishop Harold's farmhouse was half the size of Jesse's and in need of paint. Sheep and a couple of cows huddled beneath an overhang from the barn. Everything looked clean in the snow, but I wondered if the place was as run-down as it appeared.

I understood why families might secretly pray not to win the lottery to become a bishop.

I saw faces peering out the windows as we pulled into the barnyard. I wondered how often this Amish family saw a strange vehicle muscling its way through the snow and parking at their back door.

"You might as well get this over with." Brett looked in the mirror at Jesse. "You want me to go in with you?" He spoke as if addressing a child.

Jesse got out as a beautiful young Amish woman with a shawl around her shoulders came out of the back door. Her hair was a striking copper red under her white cap, with curls sneaking out. She hesitated for a moment, then strode toward Jesse with graceful steps. I was surprised that no one accompanied her, but what did I know about Amish customs? Next to zilch.

She and Jesse spoke to each other in Pennsylvania Dutch at first, but lapsed into English.

"What are you doing here?" she said. "I get the picture. You don't want to marry me."

"Just as well. All this snow would make it difficult for guests to come."

"Maybe forever?" she shot back. "Fine with me." In spite of the cold, her cheeks filled with crimson. "You never wanted to marry me anyway. You don't love me."

"And you don't love me."

In the truck, we sat like marble statues, staring straight ahead, pretending not to hear them over the hum of the engine and the whirring of the heater's fan.

"I will be out of town for a few days," Jesse told her.

"Over Christmas?"

"No, I'll be back by then. I'll stop by on Second Christmas if you like."

I'd have to ask Betsy what Second Christmas was later. I wondered how my friend felt about what we were hearing, but that would have to wait too.

"Guess we should leave," Jesse said.

"Are you sure? I'm in no hurry." She glanced back at the house.

"Yah, I'm sure. We have nothing more to say to each other." He spun around and dove into the back seat next to Betsy.

I felt empathy for Naomi. I struggled to keep my thoughts to myself with success.

Brett's hands dropped from the steering wheel. "I think you're making a mistake, Jesse."

"And what makes you such an expert?"

Brett pressed his lips together and buckled his seat belt. As we drove out of the barnyard, Jesse looked over his shoulder at Naomi, who still stood outside in the cold.

A few minutes later, we left Jesse at his farmhouse. "Don't forget to pick me up at nine tomorrow morning."

Brett let out a puff of air. "Unless it snows again."

"Sure, I gotcha." Jesse put up a hand and waved.

Brett pulled away as Jesse scaled his steps. "I am not going to drive through a blizzard just so he can escape his problems," he grumbled.

"We all have problems," Betsy said. "Don't forget that."

"How could I?"

CHAPTER 12

ONCE AGAIN, I wondered what Brett's deep, dark secret was. But the thought passed quickly as the rest of the afternoon flew by. Betsy and I helped Marian make Christmas cookies, another tradition I'd never done with my own family. Mom always said she couldn't cook, so why even try, and the deli down the street had the best cookies in town. When the cookies were done, we made dinner—a leg of lamb, served with homemade mint jelly, muffins from scratch, and scalloped potatoes.

We set the table, bowed our heads in prayer, then her father sliced the lamb.

"I want the end piece, please," Betsy said, and he placed it on her plate with the long-tined fork.

"Help yourself, dear," Marian said to me.

As I scooped scalloped potatoes onto my plate, I couldn't resist sampling a mouthful. I had actually made the dish myself, with only a few directions from Marian. It might be the first item I ever cooked from scratch.

I knew nothing was perfect, but Mennonite family life in Lancaster County looked pretty good to me. I wondered what it would be like to be part of this family.

We polished off a pecan pie embellished with a dollop of the best whipped cream I'd ever tasted. The best pie I'd ever had. Again. Was it all in my head?

I sat across from Brett, but his gaze never rested on my face for more than a moment. He seemed to listen as I answered Marian's questions about living in New York, but I suspected he was being polite. City life was of no interest to him.

All too soon, supper was over. The men stood and toddled into the living room. At first I was miffed but soon discovered that cleaning the kitchen was fun with these women. I could hear the deep voices of the men laughing in the living room as we carried trays of hot cider and warm cookies toward them.

"Ladies first," Brett said as he passed me a hot cider. So he did know I existed after all.

LATER THAT NIGHT, as I snuggled under the quilt, I felt the air pressure lower as a door closed somewhere in the house. My hand dropped over the side of the bed, but Piper wasn't there.

I clicked on the lamp and saw that my door was ajar. I hissed, "Piper, get back here."

Nothing.

I found the bathrobe and slippers Betsy had provided and padded out into the hallway and down the stairs. Where was my dog? In the kitchen, I found the lights on but no sign of either dog. I cracked the back door and was met with a blast of chilly air. Surely no one would go out for a walk on a night like tonight.

No sooner had I thought the words than Brett appeared around the corner of the house with Rex on his heels.

"Where's Piper?" I sounded more snarly than I'd meant to.

He blinked up at me in the doorway, then around. "She was here a minute ago." He scanned the backyard. "I thought she was right behind us."

I looked out into the dark sky and saw flakes of snow drifting by. As cold as it was, I stepped into a pair of rubber boots by the back door and wrestled on a long black coat.

Brett looked down at Rex.

"Where is she?" he asked the giant canine, who wagged his feathered tail as if initiating a game. I didn't find them funny or cute. Where was my Piper?

Brett zipped his jacket. "I'll go have a look."

"She doesn't know you and won't come to you. I have to go too."

"Come on, Rex." Brett started to walk out into the yard, but his dog paused and whimpered. "What's wrong with you?"

My brave little Piper never acted that way. Where was she?

Brett pulled a flashlight from his pocket and aimed it into the snowy woods. He paused and seemed to hear something, then trotted off around the corner, his dog lumbering reluctantly behind him. I followed and found Rex growling, his wide head lowered and his hackles raised. He was staring at Piper, who was barking frantically at four other dogs.

"Coyotes," whispered Brett, holding up a hand for me to stop.

"They wouldn't attack a dog, would they?" I asked him, suddenly encompassed by fear.

"They will if they're hungry enough." And with that, Brett raised his arms and charged at the wild animals, letting out a guttural sound and waving wildly at them. Rex raced after him.

Like ghosts, the coyotes shrank back into the bushes without a fight.

Piper dashed toward me. I scooped her up and ran for the back door. "What would I do if anything happened to you?" I said, followed by a sob.

When we were safely back in the kitchen, I turned and impulsively hugged Brett. "Thank you for saving her."

His arms slid around my shoulders. "My pleasure," he said.

I leaned back and gazed into his eyes, two deep pools where his secrets lived, but they revealed nothing. On an impulse, I kissed his cheek, a few inches from his mouth. I longed to kiss him for real—a languid and sumptuous kiss. Like in the movies. But of course, I didn't.

Both a little stunned, we stood in each other's arms.

"I am so sorry," he said, his strong arms supporting me. "That was entirely my fault. I saw Piper's leash but didn't think to put it on her. What an idiot."

I wanted to give him the benefit of the doubt, to tell him that no, it wasn't his fault. Piper should have come when I called her. I glanced over to see my darling dog scarfing down kibble, once again as happy as could be. I tried to pull my act together, but I was still weak at the knees.

"What's going on?" Betsy asked, startling both of us. I stepped out of Brett's arms and felt a sudden loss.

"I was a dummy," Brett said and told her what happened with Piper and the coyotes.

"I see." Betsy filled her water glass at the sink and tossed her brother a wry smirk. "Excuse me if I'm interrupting anything."

She obviously was.

CHAPTER 13

"I DON'T WANT YOU driving on those icy roads," Sam said to Betsy the next day.

"I'll be right behind her in the truck," Brett told him.

"Most of them have been cleared," Betsy said. "I'll be extra careful. Don't worry." She glanced to the ceiling. "Cousin Annie wants her car back."

Sam wagged his finger. "You shouldn't have borrowed it in the first place."

"I needed it. And I have to go back and get these final orders shipped off." She patted a pile of last-minute holiday orders waiting to be loaded in the car.

"Well, I don't want you on the road by yourself."

"Diana will be there." Betsy hesitated. "And I invited Jesse to ride with us."

Sam huffed. "Is he or is he not betrothed and about to get married?"

"I'm honestly not sure at this point," Brett said. "If so, this will be like his bachelor party."

Sam turned to Brett. "And you're staying for a couple days to give your little sister a ride home for Christmas?"

Brett nodded.

"And Diana?"

My head popped up. Brett glanced at me. "If she's invited."

Marian turned to me. "We'd love to include you, but what about your parents? Won't they miss you?"

"I'll ask them if I see them." I pushed away the sadness. "They haven't answered my calls."

"I'm sorry, honey," Marian said.

"Nothing new. But I'll probably be without a job by next week, so I'd love to come." I'd already decided to quit before my boss could fire me. I would call or text him as soon as we were back in New York.

Marian planted her hands on her hips. "I'm not saying I think this is a good idea, but if Jesse is going with you, where is he?"

"We'll swing by and get him on the way out," Betsy said.

"I think you're making a terrible mistake," Sam said. "Are you planning to join the Amish church to be with him? What's he got up his sleeve?"

"He hasn't asked me. Or told me of his plans."

Her father swiped his chin with his hand. "I never should have let you two spend so much time together growing up. All those volleyball games." He shook his head. "You are still a young woman who apparently doesn't have a clue—"

"Just remember you set up the volleyball net and invited all our neighbors over." Not bothered by her parents' disapproval, Betsy checked her wristwatch. "Got to go."

Half of me wanted to stay in the warmth of the cozy house with these amiable parents. But I'd promised that they could all stay with me in New York, and I really did need to go to the museum to gather my personal things when I quit.

"Coming?" Brett asked me.

I glanced up into his handsome face and imagined all the fun we'd have in the city. Piper circled my legs. She knew I was leaving and didn't want to be left behind. "You can come too, girlie," I told her.

In the driveway, we all agreed that I should ride with Brett to give him directions once we got to Manhattan. Betsy pulled out quickly, to get Jesse, and we loaded her packages in the back of the truck. When we finally pulled up the driveway, Brett fishtailed a little, showing off, and his tires spun in the snow.

As we reached the intersection with the road, I heard a clip-clopping, then saw a horse-drawn sleigh, tugged by two draft horses, coming up on our left.

Brett jammed on the brakes, and we skidded to a halt.

Instinctively, my arms wrapped around Piper as my seat belt locked and held me in place. We weren't close enough to have actually hit them, but in the city, horns would have blared. One horse reared up, then settled. The world stood still for a moment, then the Amish driver shook the reins, and the sleigh continued on.

I was about to shrug it all off as life in the country when I heard Brett let out what sounded like a sob. His head flopped forward against the steering wheel. "Thank the Lord," he said.

"Wow, that was close," I said with caution. What was happening?

"Too close. I was going too fast." He was clearly shaken. "Maybe we should turn back."

"Betsy could drive me home." I checked my seat belt and reached for my phone. "Want me to call her?"

He appeared in a daze.

"Brett? Are you all right?"

"I don't know what I was thinking, going so fast." He sat up and sniffed, wiping his nose with a cloth handkerchief. "Allergies."

I didn't buy it.

The engine continued to idle.

Finally, I said, "Want me to call Betsy and ask her to come back and get me?"

"Nah, she'd have a fit. Not that spending time alone with Jesse is doing her a bit of good."

"I was thinking the same thing."

CHAPTER 14

I CRADLED PIPER IN my lap. "If you change
your mind about coming to the city, I can live
with that."

"No, I want to go." Brett hesitated. "If nothing
else, I need to look after my sister."

"I can't wait to get back." Even as I said it, I imagined the clogged traffic and felt a stab of despon-
dency that my parents would probably not be there.
But I would have guests and entertainment for a
few days, and I'd be in Lancaster County again for
Christmas. "We can put up the tree and decorate
the apartment."

We rode without talking for most of the trip,
but the silence was comfortable between us. Brett
steered his pickup with skill on the crowded city
streets. It had snowed here, too, but most of the

snow had been plowed off to the side already. I directed Brett to our apartment building and noticed his awe when he saw the stately structure.

"The Upper East Side," he said. "I hear you can't get much better than this." He scanned Central Park, cloaked in snow, while we waited at a light. Kids frolicked and built snowmen. Couples strolled.

Brett's phone rang. I could hear Betsy's voice on the other end. He asked, "You know where Diana lives, right? Should we just meet you there?"

I heard her giggle. "Big brother, we're right behind you."

He looked over his shoulder and laughed.

"All right then. But where will you park in all of this traffic? Diana says there's only one extra spot in the garage."

"Don't worry. I'll figure it out."

Betsy was as comfortable driving in the city as she was in Lancaster County. I saw her snag a parking spot on the street that had just been vacated.

Brett followed my directions to the underground parking beneath our apartment building.

Piper wriggled with excitement as we dipped into the darkness. "Yup, we're home, girlie." I directed Brett to my parents' parking spots. Dad's was empty, as I expected. Would my father ever come home again?

We took the elevator straight to the seventh floor. When the doors opened, Piper led the way to our front door. I felt a flush of embarrassment when I opened the door to our luxurious apartment and imagined it through Brett's eyes. Piper had no hesitation. She scampered in as she always did, heading for the kitchen looking for food.

Brett wandered to the wide living room window. "Wow, what a view." He gazed out at the city, which looked pristine in the snow, its smudges and grit concealed. His gaze travelled south to the Plaza Hotel, then further to the Empire State Building and skyscrapers of lower Manhattan.

"Christmastime is the city at its best."

The knock on the front door set off Piper's yapping. I'd called Carlos from the car to let him know my friends would be coming, so the doorman sent Betsy and Jesse right up. They took off their snowy boots. Jesse's jaw dropped as he walked into the living room and took in its Matisse and other valuable paintings, top-of-the-line furniture, and plush carpets.

"This city is spectacular," Jesse said, his voice elevated with excitement.

"See, I told you," Betsy said.

We spent the rest of the day walking the streets of New York, gawking into store windows and shopping for Christmas presents.

"If you want to stop anywhere, tell me," I said.

"I do," Jesse said. "I want to get a haircut."

"Are you sure?" Brett asked.

"People are staring at me."

"This isn't a part of town that's known for its discount barbershops," I told Jesse. "We'll have to walk a few blocks."

"Okay, I'm used to walking." He sped up. "I can't wait."

We strolled into a neighborhood and found a small barbershop that was empty. I negotiated with the owner to get the price down. "Sure, why not?" the barber finally said. "This is a first for me. A Christmas special."

Thirty minutes later, a transformed Jesse strutted back onto the New York City sidewalk with a grin on his face and a stylish cut. He looked better than ever.

"Fantastic," Betsy said.

"It'll take some getting used to." Jesse patted his cropped hair.

"Now what?" I said.

"Should we take them to the museum?" Betsy asked me with a smirk. "If nothing else, I love their restaurant."

"Uh, I guess so." I had no reason to be afraid. "But I don't know if I can face running into Mr. Simonton. Let's wait until tomorrow."

"I agree," Betsy said. "How about if we take the subway to Ground Zero and to see the Statue of Liberty?"

Jesse's demeanor stiffened. "I don't know about riding in a subway below all those buildings."

"It'll be fine," Brett said. "Safer and faster than driving on the snowy streets."

We located the nearest subway entrance and descended the steps.

"Are you sure this is safe?" Jesse asked.

"Yes," Betsy said, "but hold on to your wallet."

"Good advice anywhere in this city," I told him.

"There are that many pickpockets?" Jesse looked over his shoulder.

I held onto my purse's strap. "Enough."

As we stood on the platform, Jesse looked across the tracks, "How do you know which train to take? What would happen if you stumbled and fell on those tracks?"

"Don't do it to find out," Brett said. "Okay?"

"Yah, I'll be careful."

The rumble of the approaching subway filled the air like an oncoming windstorm.

"What is that?" Jesse asked, dread widening his eyes.

"Just the subway, silly." Betsy looped her arm in his, then removed it.

More passengers arrived until we were shoulder to shoulder. The subway ground to its usual whining halt, and the doors parted. Passengers crammed in New York style, but Brett strode in and saved seats for Betsy and me.

I appreciated Brett's presence when a fellow, mumbling to himself, curled on the floor near us. My guess is the guy was drunk or stoned. I wondered if Brett would protect us from him, not that I wasn't used to seeing such sights. Maybe Mennonites were pacifists too.

Finally, after many stops, we reached the south end of Manhattan Island. We got out and traipsed into the colossal World Trade Center station, with its white vaulted ceiling.

"This is called the Oculus," Betsy told Jesse.

We rode the escalator up to street level. As we departed, frigid air wafting off the Hudson River accosted us. Other tourists, bundled in winter clothes, straggled along with us.

"Brrr," I said, "I should have worn warmer clothes." I led the way to admire the Statue of Liberty across the river. "On a summer's day I'd suggest we take the boat over to Ellis Island, but it's too cold today.

"The statue was a gift from the French during the American Revolution," Betsy said. She turned to Jesse. "Come back in a few months, and we can climb to the top."

"You know the history better than I do," I told her. "Guess when you grow up with something you take it for granted."

"Were you in the city on 9/11?" she asked me.

"I was just a kid, but I will never forget that day." The images on our TV were etched in my mind. "I was terrified. We all were. My mother picked me up from school early." A rare occurrence.

"For a year they were the tallest buildings in the world," Betsy said. "Ground Zero isn't far from here, if you guys want to see the memorial."

I'd just assume skip it, but I said, "Sure, I guess."

"So many lives lost," Brett said.

"War is evil," Jesse said. "What good did retaliation do?"

"We were attacked, not the other way around." I felt defensive but didn't want to get in an argument when I had no answers. I recalled watching the horrendous spectacle on TV—the commercial aircraft filled with innocent people piercing the second Twin Tower and then the tall building crumbling. My parents had told me of the many brave firemen who died while trying to save people trapped in the burning purgatory. And also strangers who had stopped to help. The city had seemed unified after the terrorist attack. After, so many of our soldiers lost their lives in Iraq in retaliation. Maybe the Amish had it right.

The snow started up again. After a brief visit to Ground Zero, we stopped in a nearby café for a warm meal. Betsy and I ordered the soup and sandwich special, and the men consumed chili.

I summoned an Uber, who headed us north to the Upper East Side. The driver dodged the chaotic motor traffic that had returned in spite of the snow. Cabbies honked their horns as vehicles and pedestrians alike muscled forward.

"You okay walking the last few blocks?" I asked my friends when the traffic came to a halt at an intersection.

"You bet, it'll be faster," Betsy said.

"Please let us out here," I told our driver. "Thanks."

We hurried to the sidewalk before the light changed—not that traffic was moving. The sidewalks were crammed with shoppers plodding through the slush. "Remember to hold onto your wallets," Betsy warned Brett and Jesse.

"Okay, Miss Know It All, we heard you the first time," Brett said.

I quickened my pace. "I hope we'll be back before Piper uses my mother's new alligator high heels as a chew toy."

A throng of people swarmed around us. A woman carrying shopping bags bumped me so hard I lost my balance. Brett caught my arm to keep me from toppling.

"How rude," he said.

"Maybe," Jesse said. "But I still think this is the most marvelous city in the world. I'd better not spend too much time here, or I won't ever want to go home."

"But your farm," Betsy said. "When the snow melts, the city will turn gray again."

I nodded. "I hate to admit how right she is."

CHAPTER 15

AS WE REACHED my building, Carlos swung
open the door for us. "Welcome home, Ms.
Manzella." He took a step back to give my entou-
rage a quick looking over. I could see them study-
ing him, too, in his forest-green suit and cap. I was
too tired to introduce him to everyone and explain
who they were.

"I don't suppose my parents are home," I asked,
already knowing the answer.

"I'm sorry, not a clue. I just came on duty a few
hours ago."

No surprise, but I still felt an ache in my chest.

I turned my thoughts to my darling Piper. She
hated being alone, and I felt guilty for leaving for
so many hours. At least now that my job was history,
I would be home much more. No, I wouldn't,

because I'd have to find another job, and it might have more hours or a longer commute.

As Betsy, Jesse, and Brett followed me down the hall, I waited to hear Piper's voice yapping, but she was silent. Probably just napping, I hoped. Even when I put the key in the lock, I heard no eruption of barking. I advanced into the living room and was shocked to see my mother lounging on the couch in a satin pantsuit. Piper slept at her feet.

"Mom—hi."

"Hello, dear." Her short beige hair was styled to perfection, as always. People said we looked alike, but I couldn't see it. She had always been the most gorgeous and vivacious woman in the room.

Piper woke up with a start and charged over to greet me with her tail wagging.

"What are you doing here?" I asked my mother.

She stubbed out her cigarette. "The last time I looked, I lived here." I was used to her snappy repartee.

"Is Dad home?"

"I have no idea where he is." She leaned to the side to look past me. "Hello, Betsy," Mom said.

"Hi, Mrs. Manzella." Mom never asked to be called by her first name.

"And who have we here?"

"My brother Brett and our friend Jesse, from Lancaster County," Betsy said.

"I hope I'm not breaking up your Christmas party. Though we could use a tree and ornaments." She turned to me. "Why don't you all put up the tree? We need some decorations and holiday spirit up here." She sipped from a brandy snifter. "Make yourself at home, everyone. Are you all planning to stay here?" She lifted her sculpted movie-star eyebrows.

"We haven't figured out the logistics," I said. "I figure Betsy can sleep in the guest room, and the men could sack out in the living room."

Mom patted the couch in a seductive manner. "This folds out into a double bed."

"That would be fabulous," Betsy said, then turned to Brett. "Wouldn't it, big brother? You're being awfully quiet." She was right. Brett looked a little dazed. My mother had that effect, especially on men.

"Are you sure it's okay, Mrs. Manzella?"

"One stipulation," Mom said. "You must put up the tree."

Jesse scanned the room. "Would we go out and buy one?"

Mom let out a girlish giggle. "You'd better not go across the street and chop one down, or you'll end up in jail."

I stepped in. "Our fake, glitzy Christmas tree lives in a cardboard box next to the washer and dryer."

Brett peered into my face as if trying to decide whether or not I was kidding.

"This is Manhattan," Betsy explained to them. "Hardly anyone uses real trees."

"Come on, I'll show you where it is. I'll need help carrying it out." I paraded everyone into the laundry room and pointed to the giant cardboard box in the corner. "It's too heavy for me by myself."

Jesse and Brett lugged the box into the living room. My mother was already on her feet, tugging one of the couches out of the way to make room. Brett smirked as he pulled the flocked tree out of the box and jimmied the three pieces together. I helped him get it on the stand and tried to see the "tree" through my friends' eyes. I felt embarrassed by its garish outline.

"It's from Hammacher Schlemmer," my mother said, as if everyone in the world had heard of the store. "If you've never been there, you really must."

"I don't think we'll have time this trip," Betsy said. Her phone chirped. She stepped out of the room for a few minutes while the rest of us studied the tree. The house phone rang, meaning a call from the doorman. Mom snagged it and said, "Perfect timing. Tell him to bring it right up." She turned and told me, "Food is on its way. Diana, how could you let the refrigerator get so empty?"

"Sorry about that," I said. "I was away—"

"No matter." Her words were silky soft, for which I was grateful. When she got mad, look out.

Betsy came back at that moment and told Brett, "That was Annie. She came to pick up her car, so I told her where to find it on the street."

I plugged in the tree; hundreds of colored LED lights sparkled to life.

Jesse stepped back. "What on earth?"

"If you don't like it, stay somewhere else," Mom snapped.

"No, no, we're grateful for your hospitality," Brett said and elbowed Jesse. "We were just surprised."

"Yah, we sure are."

A blaring siren passed below us, followed by another, accompanied by horns.

Jesse hurried to the window. "Is there a fire?"

My mother chortled. "You'd better get used to the noise, or you won't sleep a wink."

"It took me weeks," Betsy said, "but you grow used to it." I recalled the quiet at Betsy's parents' house and wished I were there.

Someone knocked on the front door.

"Coming," I called and went to get the bags from the delivery driver. "Thai food?" I asked. "Thanks, Mom."

"Oh, that looks and smells delicious," Brett said.

"I'll put some of these groceries away." Betsy scooped up a bag of fruit and vegetables and headed for the kitchen. Jesse followed, carrying a box of bottled and canned beverages. I noticed a bottle of what appeared to be champagne.

As I passed Mom, I asked her again, "Is Dad coming home tonight?"

"I don't have the slightest idea, but it's unlikely. Your father comes and goes as he pleases."

CHAPTER 16

THE NEXT MORNING we had coffee and a light breakfast of toasted bagels and cream cheese. No use trying to compete with Marian's fabulous meals. My mother slept in, as usual. I noticed a bottle of Scotch and an empty glass on the counter. My guess was she'd waited up, hoping my father would show up.

The four of us headed out on foot to the Metropolitan Museum. I tried to dissuade Betsy, but she had insisted.

"I want Brett to see where I worked," she'd said.

Brett lowered his brows. "*Worked* sounds like past tense."

"If Diana gets canned, I'll quit too."

"Oh, Betsy, don't give up your job just for me," I said.

"I've been building my quilt business. And working at the museum without you would be a drag."

"Life is more than fun and games," Brett said.

"Thanks for the reminder brother dearest."

To avoid their sister-brother squabble, I fell in next to Jesse, who surprised me by professing he'd always wanted to come to this museum. "It's on my bucket list," he said.

"Seriously?"

"Just because I attended school only through the eighth-grade doesn't mean I don't read. And dream."

"I'm sorry." I felt like a heal. "I can tell you're intelligent."

"I bet I could pass that dumb old GED test and get accepted into college."

"Is that what you want to do?" I asked.

"I don't know anymore."

We wended our way along the sidewalk—mostly cleared but icy in spots. After thirty minutes, we stood at the entrance to the majestic Metropolitan Museum. I was not excited to go in. Quite the opposite. A wave of trepidation engulfed me. What would I do and say if I saw Mr. Simonton?

At the entrance we paused to admire the ornate stone facade with its towering Corinthian columns. We climbed the museum's many front steps and entered the lobby.

Betsy turned to Jesse. "What's your favorite period of art?"

He wore a blank expression for a moment, then, to my surprise, said, "The Italian Renaissance." I don't know what I was expecting, but it wasn't that. Proving me to be a snob.

"How about you?" I asked Brett.

"Is this the museum that has the structures from ancient Egypt? If so, I'd like to see them."

"Yes, on the first floor." The Egyptian display was dangerously near the gift shop, but I shook off my fears. My fate was already sealed.

"Let's go to see Egypt first, then have a bite to eat," Betsy said. "After Egypt we can see the Italian Renaissance."

We wandered through the tall rooms full of Egyptian artifacts, some of them no doubt stolen from the Middle East. Or was I jaded to think so? The museum could have purchased these displays legally, as it had most of its works of art.

My mother had been a trustee here for as long as I could remember, so I knew this humongous museum well. I could be a docent and give tours, but today I was content to move at a snail's speed behind Brett and Jesse, who were both amazed by the grandeur of the floor-to-ceiling displays. I'd visited the museum my whole life, and I tried to see everything anew through Brett's and Jesse's eyes.

Finally, Betsy announced "I'm famished" and steered us to the elevator. On the fourth floor, we stepped into the restaurant. We all ordered chicken marsala after Betsy and I assured them the alcohol in the Marsala wine had burned off in the oven while cooking.

"Stop worrying," Betsy told Brett. "As if you two never drink beer together?"

"Well, we shouldn't," Brett said. "They don't call booze 'fire water' for nothing."

After we'd eaten and paid, Betsy said, "I've had enough. My feet are killing me."

"I agree," I said. "I can't wait to take off my shoes."

"But we haven't seen everything." Jesse scanned the map he'd picked up at the entrance.

"You'll have to come back," Brett said. "This place is too big for a single day."

"I'll stay with him," Betsy said.

"Then I'd getter stay too," Brett said. "Exactly which painters do you want to see, Jesse?"

"Botticelli and Raphael."

I knew the museum well enough to know it lacked the most famous masterpieces by those two artists. "You may have to fly to Florence or Rome to find what you're looking for."

"But I am forbidden from riding in an airplane." Jesse looked defeated.

I lacked the energy but said, "Okay we'll all have a quick look through that section."

An hour later, Jesse said his eyes and brain were too tired to view another painting. "Ach, so much nudity," he said, as we exited.

"What were you expecting?" Brett asked him.

"If you knew why didn't you stop me?"

Brett chuckled. "When have I ever had luck giving you advice?"

"Okay, we all agree we've had enough?" I said, and received a unanimous affirmative.

After retrieving our coats from the coat check, I led us out the front door.

On the street, we saw an aged horse pulling an open carriage, offering rides to tourists.

"That's a sorry looking nag," Jesse said.

"Poor thing," I said. "There's too much snow for him to be out here." Each step the horse took seemed monumental. But as I spoke, a couple flagged the driver down and climbed in.

"Make you miss Midnight?" Brett asked Jesse.

"I'm torn between missing him and wanting to be here."

When we were back at the apartment—and Mom was out of earshot—I told my friends, "You've probably figured out by now . . ." My throat constricted, trapping my words. "I might as well tell you, my parents are headed for divorce court."

"We Amish do not believe in divorce," Jesse said.

"How do you stop it?" I was taken aback by his confident tone.

"It's against the *Ordnung* and the teachings of the Bible. Against everything we believe in."

"So that's why you're not marrying Naomi?"

"In part." His features grew tense. "The idea of a lifetime commitment scares me to death. And then I found out she's seeing another man on the side."

"More than just seeing him, apparently." I knew how playing the fool felt. "She never gave you any hints?"

Jesse kneaded the back of his neck but didn't answer.

I understood many men like Jesse had problems making commitments. Was that Brett's big secret too? No, what I'd witnessed when he almost hit that sleigh was more than a commitment problem. His troubles lay deep.

CHAPTER 17

M Y MOTHER JOINED us at the dinner table. We were all enjoying take-out deli food when we heard a key in our front door lock. Piper raced to the door and yipped. A man spoke to her, sending her into ecstasy.

"Dad?" I steeled myself. Maybe it was just a cleaning person or another delivery man.

My mother swiveled to see the door. Her face lit up. "Darling, it's you."

"It looks as though you're doing fine without me." My father strolled into the dining room and removed his jacket and scarf.

"Hey, Dad, that's not true." I stood and gave him a hug. "My friends are visiting New York for a couple of days from Lancaster County. Come join us."

He harrumphed. "Well, maybe for a minute."

I introduced him to Betsy, Brett, and Jesse. "They're spending the night."

"Not sleeping in my bed, I assume."

"Of course not, darling," my mother said.

Darling? I couldn't recall the last time she had called him a term of endearment, and now she'd said it twice. Maybe having guests here was a good influence on her. On both of them, because Dad was acting his most charming self too.

When my father finished eating, he tidied up the corners of his mouth. I wanted to do something to keep him from taking off, but what? Betsy and I cleared the table and carried the dirty dishes to the kitchen.

"What can I do to keep him here?" I asked her.

"Don't turn on the TV," she said as she filled the dishwasher. "All the men will get sucked in."

"Then what?"

"Start a board game,"

"As in Scrabble or checkers?" I wondered if my mother had kept my childhood games.

"We love to play them after dinner, or any time, really. And Jesse will enjoy it." She sent me a pretty smile that told me she would enjoy watching Jesse.

I returned to our small dining area and was pleased to see so many people filling the space.

"Anyone want to play a board game?" I turned to my mother. "Do you know where they are?"

"Oh dear, maybe in the hall closet?" She seemed nervous. "I keep meaning to clear this place out."

"Are you thinking of downsizing?" Betsy asked her.

Mom shrugged and glanced at my father, as if waiting for him to put the divorce papers on the table right in front of everyone. Instead, he extracted a small box from his pocket. "Before you start taking things out, here's something to add." He placed it on the table in front of my mother, who looked surprised, her jaw dropping.

"Well, aren't you going to open it?" he asked.

My mother hesitated. "Is it something I should save for Christmas?" He shook his head, and finally, she unhinged a black velvet box to expose a pair of aquamarine earrings surrounded by diamonds. The room went silent as she examined the exquisite jewelry.

"Darling, these will match the necklace you gave me a couple years back." Her voice was exuberant.

"And the color of your eyes," he said.

I hadn't heard my father speak so tenderly to her since . . . well, forever. I noticed her eyes tearing up and felt mine doing the same.

"I adore them," she said. "And you. I adore you. I've missed you so much."

As if they were in a Hollywood movie, they both stood and embraced each other, forgetting all about us. Of course, none of my friends could begin to understand what these two had gone through over the years.

"I'll finish cleaning up the table," I said, scooting past them. Betsy followed.

Mom never looked at us. Instead, she took Dad's hand and led him toward their bedroom. "We need to talk," she purred. I couldn't remember the last time I'd seen a loving gesture between them and wondered how she would be able to forgive him. My father had acted like a cad. Not that she'd been Madam Perfect.

"Now what?" Brett said in my ear. "Do your parents want privacy? Should we leave for home tonight?"

"No, it's too dark and dangerous to drive back this late." I glanced outside and noticed white flakes twirling past. "The roads will be icy, no doubt."

"I agree." Betsy touched my shoulder. "But isn't it wonderful?"

"Yes." I was still on edge, waiting for raised voices emanating from their bedroom. But all was quiet.

"A Christmas miracle?" Brett said.

"You have no idea."

Piper stood at the front door and whined. "Her signal she needs to go out," I said. "Let's all go for a walk to the park." As we retrieved our coats, I saw Jesse pause in front of the wall mirror to admire his hair.

"You like being an Englisher?" Brett said in a teasing voice.

"Is my hair a problem with you now too?"

Brett raised his hands, palms turned up. "Hey, it's your life."

"I'll keep that in mind." Jesse narrowed his eyes.

"Shush, you two." Betsy looped her scarf around her neck.

Piper, her ears pricked and her tail wagging, seemed elated to have so much company. She pranced in place at the end of her leash.

"Okay, I'm coming, girlie." I made sure I had my key and slid into my camel-colored cashmere coat and a knit hat.

Piper yanked on her leash all the way to the park. The evening dog walkers were making their rounds. The air was alive with barking and growling, combined with children's laughter and snowballs flying.

As Piper leaped to greet a standard poodle I recognized from our walks, I felt a tug on Piper's leash. A stranger wearing a hoodie had grabbed the leash and ripped it out of my hand so hard my arm felt out of its socket. In a flash, the young man and my dog were gone.

"Hey, get back here," Brett yelled at the man, who was booking it toward the darkness in the center of the park.

"Piper, come," I called, hoping to hear her bark. Nothing.

"Can you call the police?" Betsy asked.

"I doubt it," I said. "They have their hands full with more important things."

Brett, Jesse, Betsy, and I decided to fan out, looking for Piper, and meet again in thirty minutes. I took Jesse's phone number. "It may come in handy," I told Brett and Betsy. Neither of them appeared pleased with my request.

I set off in the direction the guy had gone, feeling hopeless until I saw movement. I dashed toward a snow-covered rock, only to realize that what I'd seen wasn't Piper, but a sleeping homeless man.

My footsteps woke him up with a start. "Spare change?" he asked, his voice gruff and slurred. His breath reeked of liquor. I thought about how my parents always warned me not to wander too far into the park by myself. All sorts of people lingered in the darkness, out of sight.

I spun away from the sleeping man but walked right into another fellow, who grabbed my wrist.

"Let go of me." I tried to sound firm, but my voice was shaking. I was about to scream when I saw Brett trudging my way, looking for Piper. I had never been so happy to see someone.

Brett gathered speed when he saw me. "Let go of her this instant."

"Or what?"

"I'll call the police."

"You think New York's finest will give a rip about you?"

Using all my strength, I took advantage of the distraction and wrestled myself free. My feet slipped in the slushy snow before I got to Brett. I landed on my knees. He reached down and practically dragged me away to safety.

I wanted to hug him and thank him profusely, but Piper was still missing. "Have you seen my dog?" I asked.

"I saw half a dozen dogs playing in an open field, but I couldn't make her out."

Still holding my hand, he guided me toward the brightly lit edge of the park. I looked up and saw him glancing my way. But he didn't say a word.

Brett took me to where he'd seen dogs of various breeds and sizes frolicking and barking, having the time of their lives. But no Piper. We zigzagged across the park. "It's over eight hundred square acres," I said, feeling exhaustion blanket me.

"Where could she be?" Brett asked me. "Would she go home?"

I imagined her crushed under the wheels of a taxi cab or taken to a stranger's place. I'd heard of people stealing dogs and then demanding a ransom. I would gladly pay it.

"Does she have an ID tag on her collar?" he asked.

"Yes. It even says *Reward*. I'll call my mother."

Her phone rang so many times I didn't think she was going to answer. Finally, she said hello.

"Please tell me Piper is with you," I said. "Someone yanked her leash right out of my hand and stole her."

"Sorry, dear." She yawned. "She isn't with us." I could hear my father's chuckle in the background. Mother giggled. She was laughing? Oh dear, I was interrupting them.

"Mom, we're going to head home and hope that somebody finds her and reads her tag. I'm sorry if we're interrupting anything."

"Sweetheart, I already told you your friends are welcome, so don't worry about it."

First darling, now sweetheart?

"Thanks, Mom." I wondered about bringing my crew back to our place, but we had to be there in case Piper showed up.

I scanned the lofty buildings surrounding the park. Suddenly this city seemed like the worst place on earth to live. I was seized by panic.

"We'd better find Betsy and Jesse," Brett said, tapping his cell phone. A moment later his phone chimed, and he read the message. "They're together and headed this way."

My cell phone chirped with my mother's signature message tone. "Piper is here."

Ten minutes later, the four of us arrived at my building. Carlos greeted us. "I saw some jerk walking down the sidewalk with your pooch," he said.

"Was he looking for us?"

"Nah. In fact, I had to struggle to get him to let go of Piper's leash. Get this. He threatened to call the police. What a hoot. I threatened to do the same thing, until finally he dropped the leash and ran down the sidewalk."

Carlos would be getting an extra-large Christmas bonus this year.

"Thank you so much. Where is she now?"

"Your father came down to fetch her a few minutes ago."

Piper was waiting for me at our front door. Her feet pranced with delight. I bent down to scratch her behind the ears and felt her damp fur. She licked my fingertips.

Jesse let out a huff. "This city is a terrible place to keep a dog." I couldn't disagree with him. He went to take off his coat and then exclaimed, "*Ach,* my pocket is empty." He dug his hand in to double check. "My wallet is gone."

"I warned you," Betsy said, hands on her hips.

"I was careful. I only stopped once to talk to a man who was lost and needed directions. Should I go back and look for it? Maybe I dropped it."

"If you did, it's gone by now," I told him.

"But I recall the man. I've got to try to look for him." He ducked back into the elevator.

"Wait," I called out. "How will you find your way back here?"

"I'd better go with him," Betsy said and slipped into the elevator just as the doors closed.

"I should go with her," I told Brett, reaching for my coat.

"And leave me here alone with your parents?" Brett said. "No thanks."

My mind swam with visions of awkward encounters. I nodded. "Okay, we'd better both follow them."

CHAPTER 18

I LED BRETT TO the fire escape stairway. We dashed down, reached the ground floor in time to see Jesse and Betsy leaving the building and blending into the throng.

Brett shouted, "Betsy!" and his sister turned in surprise. Jesse kept going.

"You're on a fool's mission," Brett said when we caught up with her. "Even back home—"

Tires screeched outside. We all turned to the street and watched helplessly as a limousine struck Jesse, who crumpled to the ground. The driver, a middle-aged black man dressed in a suit and cap, jumped out as we raced to Jesse's side.

"You okay?" the driver said but got no response. Jesse wasn't moving, although I could see he was breathing and there was no visible blood. The driver was a hulk in stature, but he didn't try to move him. "Hey, buddy, can you hear me?"

"Jesse," Betsy said, her voice urgent. "Jesse, wake up."

After several long seconds, Jesse's eyes blinked open, and his fingers wiggled.

"Need a ride to the hospital?" the driver asked. "I just dropped my fare off. Plenty of room."

Horns honked behind the limo; the driver signaled them to progress around him. It wasn't an easy feat, I noticed, with the big piles of snow pushed to the sides of the street.

"I'm okay," Jesse said without enthusiasm.

"Are you sure?" Betsy asked. "Can you move your feet and legs?"

"I can take him to the nearest emergency room," the driver said again. "No problem."

Jesse pushed himself up to a sitting position. "Really, I'm all right. Just had the wind knocked out of me."

Horns continued to blare. "I'd better get my car out of the way." The driver handed me his business card. "But like I told you, I could take him to the nearest emergency room if you think anything is broken."

"Just bruised." Jesse said again but accepted the driver's help getting to his feet.

"What were you thinking, running out in the street like that?" I asked, while Betsy dusted snow and grit from his jacket.

"Guess I wasn't thinking at all. Are there always this many cars on the street?"

"Yes." Betsy and I said in unison.

"Even in the snow?"

"Yes."

Betsy looked like she had plenty more to say but remained quiet. As we returned to the apartment's front door, she slipped her arm around Jesse's waist. Brett steadied him from the other side. "I think we've had enough excitement for one day."

"Yah."

"I can't believe you just ran into the street without looking," I said.

"Diana, give the man a break," Brett said. "You sound like our mother."

I squared my shoulders. "I take that as a compliment. I like your mother."

"And I like yours."

CHAPTER 19

WHEN WE GOT back upstairs, we made Jesse comfortable in a reclining chair and covered him with a mohair blanket. He continued to assure us he was perfectly fine and resisted suggestions of seeing a doctor, but I knew he could have a concussion and not know it. I explained to the group what I'd read somewhere—that we should wake him every two hours.

"I'll sit out here with him," Betsy said, and Brett scowled.

"What's wrong?" She glared back at him. "You don't trust me to take care of him?"

"I've seen the power Jesse has over women."

"Hey, too loud, Brett," Jesse mumbled. "You're giving me a headache."

"You have a headache?" I asked. "Maybe you do need to go to the hospital."

Jesse's hands moved to cover his ears. "There's nothing wrong with me that a good night's sleep and a day of rest won't cure."

"You're tired of the city already?" Brett ask him.

Jesse yawned. "I am too tired to play your mind games." He lay the side of his head against the seat back. "Let me sleep."

"Are you sure he needs to be woken up every two hours all night?" Brett asked me.

"I read it in an article somewhere, but I'm not a medical doctor."

Betsy pulled out her phone. "I'll Google it." She was quiet for a few minutes, reading, her brows furrowed. "Yes, Diana's right."

"I'd say we're all in for the evening, don't you think?" Brett said to me.

"You and Diana can go out, and I'll stay behind," Betsy said. "I don't mind."

"I don't think so." I said. "What if Jesse gets worse?"

I TOSSED IN a sea of sheets and blankets all night. Each time I floated to the surface of wakefulness,

I heard voices. Several times, it sounded like Betsy and Brett arguing. And Jesse? I wondered if he was awake but decided to stay put rather than get in the middle of a brother-sister spat.

The next morning as I brewed coffee, I found myself hoping it would be to Brett's liking. Jesse lay snoring on the foldout couch. I was happy to find him less attractive than I had before. What had I been thinking, even giving him a second glance? If Jesse came on to me, he might be shunned. It was bad enough he'd gotten his hair cut, which would irritate the bishop. I shouldn't care what Bishop Harold thought of me, but I did.

And Brett? He might only be indulging me so he could look after his sister. I appreciated him for that. But he harbored some sort of secret. After Vince, I'd vowed to steer clear of men with double lives.

Piper rubbed against my legs and begged for breakfast. After her adventure in the park last night, I imagined she was starving. I thought again about how I might have lost my darling girl forever. I shuddered. Some people might find me loony for loving a dog so much, but I did. I filled her bowl with her favorite kibble, and she dove in with gusto.

My mother strolled out of my parents' bedroom wearing a floor-length robe. "I smell coffee." She sniffed the air and smiled. "Do you have enough extra for us?"

"Sure, just made a fresh pot." I tried not to stare at her smudged mascara as I pulled out a couple of extra mugs. "Help yourself."

She blushed. "I thought I'd bring your father breakfast in bed. We haven't done that for years."

The guest room shower had been running; I heard it snap off. "That must be Brett," I said.

"You two would make a charming couple. If he lived in the city, that is."

What was she getting at?

"He's my friend's brother, Mother. Nothing more. And he doesn't live in the city."

She shrugged one shoulder. "Don't bite my head off. I was merely making an observation."

She was an expert at drawing the truth out of me, but when it came to Brett, I didn't know the truth. When it was clear I wasn't going to add any tidbits, she waltzed back to the bedroom, carrying two cups of coffee.

Brett appeared a few minutes later, freshly shaved and with damp hair. "That coffee smells divine."

I handed him a mug. "You're an angel," he said, making my cheeks warm.

I covered my uneasiness by busying myself. "Sugar and half-and-half are on the kitchen counter." I poured myself a cup and splashed in cream from my stash in the refrigerator.

Above the kitchen sink, a small window offered a different view of Central Park under a cloudy, gray sky.

"You up for some more shopping this morning?" I asked him. I wanted to buy a few presents for his family and something to leave under the tree for my parents.

He stretched. "Not really. I have more than enough stuff at home."

Meaning that he wasn't buying a present for me? I scolded myself for even thinking about it. Why would I expect Brett to buy me a Christmas present? We hardly knew each other, and I certainly didn't need anything either. I owned clothes with the tags still on them. My lifestyle seemed so frivolous now.

Betsy was still asleep, but then again, she'd helped Brett wake Jesse every two hours, so I shouldn't complain.

"But I do think we should get Jesse home." Brett covered his mouth to yawn. "His sisters will look after him, and I'll catch up on my sleep."

"Okay, I want to do some last-minute shopping, then I'll get packed." I took a brisk shower, dressed in a turtleneck and corduroy slacks, and applied a minimum of makeup. While everyone was still sleeping or lounging around, I dashed out to a couple of local shops to buy my gifts, then hurried back to gather clean clothes and toiletries. I stuffed everything into a bulging overnight bag.

I paused at my parents' bedroom door and heard voices and laughter. I rapped lightly on the door. "Knock, knock," I said. "Is it safe to come in?"

"Yes, come in," my mother said.

I poked my head in just enough to see them both sitting on the bed, clad in bathrobes and sipping coffee. They grinned.

"We're taking off again for Lancaster County," I said.

"Whatever you like," my father said. "Don't let us keep you."

"Are you sure you don't mind me leaving?"

"Not at all." My father curved his arm around my mother's shoulder. "You head out to Lancaster County again and have fun."

"What about Piper?" I asked as the little dog trotted down the hall toward me and pranced at my feet.

"She's always miserable when you leave. Better take her."

"What will you do for Christmas?" I asked with caution.

Dad kissed my mother on the tip of her nose. "How does Chinese food sound?" he asked her.

"Scrumptious."

Was I mistaken, or had she batted her eyes at him? Whatever was happening, it was clear they didn't need their adult daughter at home watching their every move.

CHAPTER 20

TWO HOURS LATER the four of us were back on the road, traveling southwest toward Lancaster County. The remains of the storm could still be seen all around us, with semis and cars resting willy-nilly at the side of the road. Tow trucks labored to assist them.

"What are your plans?" I asked Jesse as we exited the highway and got closer to his home.

"I'm not moving to the Big Apple, if that's what you're asking. Too hectic. Too many people. And in just one night, someone almost stole your dog, and someone took my wallet."

"That's only half my question." I didn't want to come off as nosy, but I wanted to know what was in store for him. "Are you marrying Naomi?"

Brett slowed the truck and pulled into the parking lot of a clock shop, of all things. He turned to Jesse. "Good question. Are you planning to marry Naomi or not? I'm not sure she really knows."

"Yes, I am." Jesse said without conviction.

"Seriously?" I said.

"Have you given her a clock?" Brett asked.

"Not yet."

"Well, look where we are. You have my pickup at your disposal, so let's select one right now."

"A clock is like an engagement present," Betsy told me. "An Amish custom."

"I don't know," Jesse said, but Brett killed the engine and set the parking brake. He was a man on a mission. "Come on, we'll all help you choose the best one."

"Are you sure?" I asked Brett.

"Yes, I'm sure," Brett said. "Jesse has kept Naomi dangling long enough. It's time to step up to the plate." He opened the door and looked at his sister in the back seat. "You coming, too, Betsy?"

"If I have to." We all piled out of the vehicle, Brett leading and Betsy lagging.

We entered the small shop, and the proprietor, a middle-age balding man wearing what I now knew to be English clothes, greeted us. I marveled over the array of wooden clocks, realizing that they were all windup or battery operated, created specifically for Amish houses.

Much to my surprise, Jesse got down to business. He looked around for only a few minutes, then zeroed in on a clock as tall as me. I could imagine the stately clock chiming the hour in Jesse's home. "This is it." He glanced to the owner. "But I have no money with me."

"Not a problem." Brett extracted his wallet, pulled out a credit card, and handed it to the proprietor. As the man rang up the transaction, Brett told Jesse, "I'll lend you the money. No, hold on, please accept this as a wedding gift."

"Oh—okay." Jesse kept his gaze glued to the clock. "Thanks, Brett, but it's so expensive. Over one thousand dollars."

"What's the use of having money if I can't spend it on a gift for my best friend?"

The owner bundled the clock in brown paper and plastic bubble wrap and thanked Brett, then helped the men place it gently in the pickup's bed. Betsy watched the procedure, then turned to Jesse. "Is my brother forcing you into something you don't want to do?"

"Betsy," Brett said, "please let it go."

But Betsy had a point. I turned to him. "Jesse, are you sure this is what you want to do?"

He didn't answer. "Brett, this doesn't feel right. It's like a shotgun wedding."

Brett set the truck in reverse. "Jesse is not a child." We rolled back onto the snow-covered road and followed a horse and buggy toward home. "Although he's been acting like one."

Brett stared at the buggy. We drove in silence for ten minutes.

"I can't wait for Naomi to see her clock," Jesse said, in an unexpected burst of enthusiasm.

"Well then, I'll take you there right now." Brett flipped on his turn signal and took a left.

"No, not right now," Jesse said, deflating as quickly as he'd gotten excited. "I'm not ready."

"I disagree." Brett stepped on the gas. "We have the clock right here with us, so why put off the inevitable?"

"It's not inevitable if he doesn't wish to marry her," Betsy argued.

"You're right," Jesse said. "Let's go and get this over with. I don't want to hitch up Midnight and bring it over by myself later." Still, when we reached Bishop Harold's barnyard, Jesse lingered in the truck. "I thank you for the ride, Brett." He seemed to be moving in slow motion as he turned to me. "And please thank your parents for their hospitality, Diana."

"I will."

The back door opened, and out stepped the bishop, followed by the deacon and Naomi. Jesse took a deep breath and got out of the truck.

Bishop Harold crossed his arms as he surveyed Jesse's new haircut. "Are you leaving the church?"

"No." Jesse reached up and touched his cropped hair, as if he'd forgotten it was short. "My hair grows very quickly. It won't take long." He walked to the end of the truck. "I brought Naomi something."

A smile bloomed on her face as she stepped around her father and toward Jesse. "Show me." I saw her catch herself and glance back into her father's grim face to make sure her actions were all right with him.

"Yah, go ahead and have a look." The bishop seemed as interested as his daughter.

"Will you please help me?" Jesse asked Harold. The two men reached into the pickup truck's bed, took hold of the package, and held the gift out to her. She paused a moment, then unwrapped it.

"A clock?" She giggled and jumped up and down.

"The most beautiful clock in Lancaster County." Jesse glanced into her face, then looked away. Naomi appeared as if she would throw herself into Jesse's arms, but she lowered her head instead. Her father studied the clock, nodded, and patted Jesse on the back. "Are you planning to grow out your hair and wear a hat? And toss away the cell phone and the car you think no one knows about?"

"Yes, as soon as I get home. I just didn't want to wait another minute to give Naomi her gift."

"And we'll see you at church on Sunday?"

"Yah."

"Even if it requires a kneeling confession before the congregation?"

Jesse's face blanched. "Yah, okay. I'll be there."

Naomi's eyes sparkled with delight, although Jesse's face remained sober.

The conversation wound down quickly. To my surprise, a few minutes later we were all back in the cab and driving away. "I'll come back and visit her tonight, when her family is sleeping," Jesse told me. "Then she and I can speak more openly."

"Won't her parents mind?" I asked.

"No, they'll expect it."

"Seriously?" I was struck by how little I knew about Amish customs and traditions.

Brett nodded, but Betsy remained motionless. "Maybe you'll change your mind before that."

"And chicken out again?" Jesse asked. "No, it's too late for all that."

"I don't understand why you're marrying her," I said. "Not to say you shouldn't."

"I promised my *dat*."

Brett patted my knee. "Let's not talk him out of doing the right thing." Minutes later he pulled to a crunching stop in Jesse's barnyard; the young Amishman got out. No one said a word.

I lowered my window; the cab filled with a swoosh of bitter cold air. "Goodbye, Jesse." I figured I would never see him again.

The back door of his house burst open, and his sisters skittered down the stairs chattering in Pennsylvania Dutch to their brother.

"What are they saying?" I asked Brett.

"Apparently, Naomi called some friends from their phone shanty and spilled the beans. Her mother is gathering local Amish women to start scrubbing the bishop's house in preparation for the wedding."

"They'll get married in her home?" I asked. "Not in a church?"

"Yep, or in a barn if the weather turns warm. But it won't until May. Everyone in the district—including the children—will be invited, plus a few English friends like our family."

"But by tomorrow they could split up." Betsy sounded peeved. "Or anything could happen."

Brett sighed. "Are you determined to break your own heart?"

"Since when did you become Mr. Perfect?" Betsy's grief turned to spitefulness. "How about if I tell Diana about your broken heart?"

"Shush," Brett said. "Or you'll find yourself walking home."

Of course I wanted her to prattle on, but I acted as though my name had not been mentioned.

"What is wrong with you?" Brett said after a pause. "I haven't forgotten what happened. I never will. But Betsy, you've been chasing after Jesse your whole life. You're making a fool of yourself."

"Wait!" Jesse stood at his back door and beckoned us to come in the house.

Piper yipped.

"What do you think?" Brett asked me. "Had enough adventures for the day?"

I had no answer for him. After a sleepless night, I was ready to go back to bed, but curiosity wormed into me.

The snow started up again. "I'm glad we're almost home," Brett said, as if reading my mind, "but I wouldn't mind a short visit and some of Jesse's sisters' baked goodies. Not to mention another cup of coffee."

"Sure, let's go in," Betsy said. "What could a few more minutes matter?"

CHAPTER 21

As Betsy climbed out of the back seat, Brett's phone chimed. "Hold on, it's Dad," he said. He read the message. "We need to head home pretty soon."

"How about in fifteen minutes?"

"Maybe . . ." Brett glared at her. His voice became insistent. "Never mind, get in this minute. I'm done chauffeuring you around the county. I haven't heard one note of gratitude from you."

"Don't have a cow." Her face pinched, she got back into the pickup.

"Don't act like this in front of a guest."

"Diana is no guest. She's my best friend."

I was? I tried to imagine who my best friend was and couldn't think of anyone I cared for more than Betsy.

His lips pressed together, Brett glanced over at me.

"You know, if you two would just get married, everything would be perfect," Betsy said. "Diana and I really would be sisters."

"Don't be ridiculous." Brett's neck bent as he watched a vulture circling a field.

"You're the one who's being ridiculous."

I felt my cheeks flooding with embarrassment. Betsy was acting goofy, wasn't she? What was I expecting, for this handsome Mennonite man to fall head over heels in love with me, while all this time I'd been keeping one eye on him and one on Jesse?

No one spoke as we pulled down Jesse's driveway and up to the Yoder house. The snow had started again, accumulating on the windshield. "We made it home just in time," Betsy said.

"And to think I almost left you there," Brett replied, and the tension lightened.

"You wouldn't dare." Betsy smiled and punched him on the shoulder. Brother and sister were back to their old form.

"Do that again, and I'll take you back to Jesse's house."

"You would?" She grinned. "Maybe I'll take you up on that offer."

"Forget it." Brett drove around the house to the back door and set the parking brake. He sat still in the driver's seat for a long second. I wondered if he was still irritated. Or hurting. Whatever it was, I wished I could help him.

"Let me out," Betsy demanded, pushing her shoulder to open her door. She slammed it again. In a flash, she disappeared into the curtain of snow.

Brett and I sat there for several minutes with the engine running, the heat swirling around our legs. Betsy's words stuck in my mind. I didn't want to go inside yet.

I touched his hand. "Do you want to tell me about what happened? If not, I'm okay with whatever. Your problems are none of my business." I realized that came out wrong. "If you have a problem, I'm willing to listen."

Another long pause filled the pickup's cab.

"Okay." Brett worked his mouth, stroked his chin. "Years ago, when I first got my driver's license, I hit a horse and buggy." He turned to me, his features filled with the look of remorse.

I waited.

"Two people died, and it was my fault entirely." Still, I waited.

"It was Jesse's mother and his younger brother." His voice sounded choked, as if he were having trouble breathing. "They died because of my negligence."

"Oh, how terrible." I couldn't help myself from saying. In my mind's eye, I envisioned a gruesome tragedy. "And the horse?"

"It died too. I'll spare you the gory details."

I pushed the image away. "But you and Jesse are still friends."

"Jesse forgave me immediately, as did his father and his sisters." Brett's eyes filled with tears, but he held his emotions in. "The whole Amish community forgave me, in fact, but I can't forgive myself. I carry a heavy lead apron over my shoulders every day. And Jesse was never the same after the accident. He was a boy who needed a mother. His father barely paid him any attention. We didn't know about his cancer at the time, but he died just a year later. His dad had held back the news to spare the family more grief."

I let my head fall against the headrest and imagined what it must have been like for both families. I had so many questions, but now was not the time. For now, I was stuck on the idea that Jesse and the Amish community had forgiven Brett. That was beyond my comprehension.

"Now that you know, have you lost all respect for me?" He maneuvered himself to face me.

I thought carefully about my words. "I have no reason to not respect you. Quite the opposite."

My arms reached out to embrace him. He must have felt the same, because suddenly, his arms slid around me. My mouth found his for a brief kiss— the sweetest kiss I had ever experienced.

"I'm sorry," he said, pulling away. "I shouldn't have done that."

I wasn't sorry in the slightest, but before I could voice my thoughts, we heard Rex barking outside Brett's window. Piper came to life, her ears pricked and her tail wagging.

Someone stood in the snow watching us.

CHAPTER 22

"WHO'S THAT?" I asked.

"Just my dad." Brett lowered his window a couple of inches.

"Are you two okay?" Sam asked. "Your sister dashed into the house a few minutes ago but said she forgot her presents out here in your truck. She asked me to bring them in. Do you need help with anything else?"

"We're fine. Just got to talking . . ."

In spite of the frigid air, Sam grinned. "You sure there's nothing I can do to help?"

I covered my embarrassment by looking busy. "If you could hold Piper's leash and bring her into the house, that would be great," I told Sam. "I've got a bag or two."

"I can get those," Brett said. "Hey, Dad, don't let her little dog run away."

"Yes, sir."

I was pleased with the attention. "Thanks, I'll take all the help I can get." I twisted around to survey the bags in the back seat. Betsy must have been in such a hurry she forgot her overnight bag too. Poor girl. I hated to see my dear friend's heart break.

"Are you coming?" Brett asked me.

I'd been mesmerized by the falling snow and had lost track of time. "Uh, sure am." I shouldered my door open and handed Piper's leash to Sam.

"Don't worry, I've got a good hold of her." Sam gathered a bag full of the presents I'd brought. Thank goodness my closet in New York had bulged with goodies I hadn't gotten around to giving to anyone, plus all of the things I'd bought for myself but never used. Call it chronic shopping with my mother's credit card. I had closets full of unworn sweaters, purses, and jewelry—not that I'd seen a Mennonite or Amish woman wearing any. Or makeup. I had started wearing less and didn't miss it. No need to hide behind a mask.

I'd also found a men's wool scarf and a wallet that I'd planned at one time to give my father. Those, along with what I'd bought in the city, would be enough to share this Christmas. After being around the Yoders, I realized how little I needed presents. Worldly paraphernalia bogged me down.

I pictured my parents at home together in each other's arms. Their restored marriage was the only Christmas gift I really wanted or needed.

"Coming?" Sam asked.

"Yes, sorry." Snow covered the windshield; I could see only one blurry light at the back door at the top of the stairs. I reached for my belongings and followed Brett and Sam toward the house.

"Better let me carry this too." Brett hefted up my heaviest bag as if it were weightless.

Marian met me as we came through the door. "What took you so long? I started to worry."

"I'm the slowpoke." Pleased to see a pair of slippers waiting for me, I slid off my shoes in the back utility room.

"What's all this?" she asked when I came into the kitchen. She waved at the bags Sam and Brett had left in a pile.

"I couldn't come back empty-handed," I said, wondering if I'd made a mistake. I should have asked Betsy about her traditions. Did Mennonites even exchange Christmas presents? "Just a few little gifts for under the tree. If that's what the family does."

"Yes, we do, and we have loads of extra wrapping paper," Betsy said. "Mom saves it from the year before. But you shouldn't have."

"Too late now." I smiled. "You can pay me back by sharing the wrapping paper with me. And some ribbon."

"You're on. I'll put it in your room at the top of the stairs."

The words *your room* were a melody to my ears.

The house smelled luscious, better than any New York restaurant. I detected baking dough; the warmth of it filled me in a way I hadn't experienced since childhood. I was beginning to feel like part of the family. Add Brett to the mix, and I was in paradise.

Betsy was clearly not as happy. She stood staring out a window at the falling snow, her shoulders slumped. I wondered what Jesse was up to tonight. And Naomi. Was she really in love with another man? Was she happy she was getting married to Jesse?

I took hold of my overnight bag, ascended the stairs, then closed my door.

My phone chimed to let me know I had a message waiting. I froze for a moment when I saw it was from Mr. Simonton. In the rush to leave town, I'd totally forgotten that I was scheduled to work today, and I hadn't called. Before I lost my nerve, I tapped in his number. His tirade started as soon as he picked up the phone, but I interrupted. "Mr. Simonton, please forgive me for disturbing you, but I quit." I hung up, feeling nothing but relief that the inevitable had happened. I was done being a people pleaser.

I tried Jesse's phone, even though I presumed it was the wrong thing to do.

He answered and seemed surprised to hear my voice. "Everything okay?" he asked.

"You tell me. And I want the straight scoop."

He paused. "Are you asking about Naomi?"

"You know I am, so spit it out."

"Hang on. I'm on my way to the barn to feed the animals." His breathing sped up. I pictured him strolling across the snowy barnyard. I heard a horse, probably Midnight, snort and Jesse's voice soothing him.

"What's this really about, Diana?" he asked.

I made sure my bedroom door was shut before I answered. "I think Betsy deserves a straight answer about your intentions. You must know how she feels about you."

Another pause. "I don't know what you're talking about. Certainly, Betsy does not expect me to marry her. I'm engaged and about to wed someone else."

"I'm not sure she knows that." I sat on the side of the bed and tried to calm my mind.

"I never did or said anything otherwise," he said.

I considered Brett, who had never said anything to me either. Why would I assume that he cared for me? Well, at least Marian and Sam liked me, as did Betsy.

"So, you're marrying Naomi?" I asked.

"Yes. I must. I promised my father on his deathbed to marry an Amish woman. Preferably what you call a clergyman's daughter. And Naomi's not so hard to look at, yah?"

"I can't disagree. Naomi is beyond beautiful." I still had questions. "But you're willing to raise another man's child?"

"I visited her late last night. We sat in the kitchen and talked and talked." He let out a lengthy sigh. "She admitted she'd been lying about that."

"But why on earth?"

"To test my devotion to her." He paused. "Women are strange creatures, aren't they?"

I chuckled. "And men aren't?"

"Yah. But I know even if she loves another now, she will learn to love me."

I thought about that for a quiet minute and decided he was right. "When is the wedding?" I asked.

"In a few weeks, when the snow thaws and the roads are clear enough for our guests to travel safely. Her parents will arrange everything."

"May I come?"

"Certainly. But I'll warn you. It's nothing like an Englisher's wedding. There's no long white bridal gown. But it will be good." He chuckled. "One more warning, however. Be prepared to sit on a hard surface for a long time. But after the ceremony comes food."

I decided that I would be there, no matter what. I didn't want to return to New York, even if the seating was more comfortable.

Jesse and I said our goodbyes. I headed back to the kitchen to snag a warm biscuit and to see how I could help Marian with dinner. I glanced out the window. The snowflakes were multiplying.

Betsy stood setting the table, her actions slow and deliberate. I leaned in and whispered, "I called Jesse."

Her head snapped back. "You did?" Her face grew hard. She straightened the flatware. "Well, what did he say?"

"Better come with me." I led her into the back room for privacy.

A tear already rolled down Betsy's cheek. She knew what was coming. "Go ahead," she said. "Tell me all."

I hated to be the one, but she was my friend, and she deserved to know the truth.

"Jesse and Naomi are getting married in a few weeks," I blurted.

"Are you sure?" Her face turned white.

162

"That's what he told me." But that didn't make it true. "I wish I had better news." I felt salty moisture pressing at the back of my own eyes. "Maybe this is for the best."

"Easy for you to say." She blinked a succession of blinks. "Not that any of this is your fault. Brett warned me to stay away from Jesse. So did my folks."

"In that case, going to Manhattan was a smart move for you," I said. "I applaud you for it."

"I was trying to escape my love for him, for all the good it did me." Her hand flew up to cover her mouth. "Promise me you'll never repeat that."

CHAPTER 23

MARIAN ASSURED ME she didn't need help in the kitchen, so I took my biscuit upstairs and put away my clothes. Later, I followed Piper into the living room, where the Yoder family had gathered in front of the hearth. I could smell a medley of cooking vegetables, chicken, and baking dough. The room looked like the picture of tranquility, but I knew better.

"But Mom." Betsy sounded plaintive.

"We cautioned you." Sam stood and stoked the fire. "You need to start going to the church singles group again. There are plenty of fine men looking for a young woman like you. Don't wait too long."

Were we past our prime? Someday I wanted to get married and have children, but how would that happen? I glanced to Brett, whose face had soft-ened. His anger had dissipated.

Trying not to draw attention to myself, I found a comfy spot at the end of the couch. Piper tailed me in and sat at my feet, while Rex stretched out and enjoyed the heat of the fire.

"Is there anything anyone wishes to say?" Sam asked.

"Yes." Brett turned to me from the other end of the couch. "Diana, I apologize for taking my frus-tration out on you." He rubbed his hands together. "It's not your fault Jesse strung my sister along."

"Christmas is the time for reconciliation and for-giveness," Sam said, his voice filled with approval.

I glanced over to Betsy and was glad to see she was not crying.

"I forgive Jesse too," she said. "I have been such a dummy. I'm so embarrassed."

"No need to be." Marian stood and hugged her.

"Anything else?" Sam asked.

I had a kooky vision of Brett saying he was falling in love with me and that he wanted me to stay here forever. But he didn't. And why would he? He stroked Rex behind the ears, then got to his feet.

"I'm famished," Brett said. "Anything to eat?"

"We have plenty to snack on before dinner, but I don't want you to fill yourself up," Marian told him. She stood.

"Should we mosey into the kitchen?" Brett asked.

"No, not yet. I'll bring cheese and crackers out here and make you wait for the rest." Marian grinned. "I've got chicken potpie in the oven."

"That's what smells so tasty," I said. "My mouth is watering."

Betsy smiled at last. "Wait until you taste Mom's chicken potpie. She's the best cook in the county."

"I wouldn't go that far, but I'd gladly teach Diana how to make it." Marian sent me a smile. "If you wanted a lesson."

"Yes," I said. "Thank you, I would." I needed to learn how to cook. I couldn't live on takeout in Lancaster County.

I was amazed Betsy had any appetite after what she'd been through, but she popped to her feet and followed her mother into the kitchen.

I smoothed my hands over the coffee table. "I love this table," I told Sam. "Did you make it?"

"Yes. When the storm passes, we'll take you to our shop and show you around. Our specialty is hand-crafted furniture reproductions of eighteenth and early nineteenth century American styles. We also restore antique pieces."

I wondered why Betsy had never mentioned the family business.

"I'm sure glad we got our orders out before the storm and gave the crew the week off for Christmas.

Half of our employees are Amish. They're wonderful workers and skilled, but this snow would have been hard for them." Sam sat, crossed his legs at the ankles. "Someday soon Brett will run the whole business. I'm ready to retire."

"You're still young," Brett told Sam.

"I don't feel like it since my fall last summer." Sam rubbed his knee. "And you're the one who knows how to use the internet. Someday our business will rely on it."

"You can say that again." Marian returned, carrying a platter of crackers and cheese. Both dogs got to their feet and wagged their tails with expectation. "No, this is not for you."

"Cheese is bad for dogs," Betsy said. "It can make them sick."

"Not so, my little sister," Brett said. "You're thinking of chocolate."

"I don't believe that." Betsy lay a slice of cheddar on a cracker and bit into it.

"Well, it's true. And grapes and raisins very bad for dogs."

"Hey, you two, what's gotten into you?" Marian shook her head. "Our orders are completed, we're about to celebrate our Savior's birth, and you're arguing about the dogs' diet?"

I understood why Betsy was feeling snarly, but what was Brett's problem? Maybe he had a sweetheart somewhere he wanted to be spending time with. A troubling thought for me. I glanced over and admired his strong profile. In a short time, I'd grown fond of him. But how would a relationship with him ever work out?

He looked over, and our eyes locked. I was filled with a delicious warmth until he turned away as a crunching sound shattered the air outside. We all ran to the window to look at the broken branch lying in the snow.

Brett chuckled. "The snow is helping us prune."

"Could a branch fall on the roof?" I asked.

"Possibly, but I doubt it. Dad and I did major pruning over the summer to prevent such an occurrence. I'm just glad that branch didn't fall across the driveway."

"Thinking of going somewhere?" Betsy asked him.

He turned to her and glowered. "None of your business," he said, his voice firm.

"If you two are going to argue," Marian said, "you will find coal in your stockings."

CHAPTER 24

WHEN I AWOKE the next morning, I had to remind myself it was Christmas Eve—and I'd allowed myself the indulgence of sleeping in. I took a quick shower, dressed in a red turtleneck and black corduroys, and trotted down the stairs with Piper at my heels.

I smelled the dark coffee before I entered the kitchen. Marian stood at the stove fixing waffles and scrambled eggs; Sam sat at the end of the table at his usual spot.

"Good morning, dear," she said to me. "How did you sleep?"

"Like a baby. This country air must agree with me."

"Not too quiet for you?" Sam asked, then chuckled.

"Apparently not."

Betsy strolled in minutes later. "Where's Brett?" I wondered the same thing. She looked out the window. "Where's his pickup?"

"He took off about thirty minutes ago," Sam said. "Didn't say where he was headed." He sipped his coffee as I imagined Brett leaving in a huff, for reasons I didn't understand. Maybe he was going to argue with Jesse again.

Marian poured the eggs into a hot skillet. "Your brother is a grown man. You two sleepyheads take a seat so I can feed you breakfast. Susie already ate. I think she's upstairs wrapping presents."

"What I need to do," I said. "After coffee, that is."

"And breakfast," Betsy said.

"That smells so good." I inhaled the scrumptious aromas. I once again tried to recall my mother making breakfast for me, but couldn't. Hold everything, hadn't I decided to forgive her for her shortcomings? She had done plenty for me. I needed to be grateful, starting this moment.

After helping Marian clean up the kitchen, Betsy and I wrapped presents. I asked her advice about what Brett and her father would prefer.

"Give my brother the tartan plaid scarf. He'll love it this time of year, and blue is his favorite color." She examined the wallet. "Dad could really use a new wallet," she told me. "His is falling apart."

I was relieved I had chosen well, at least in Betsy's eyes. I didn't show Betsy her present, but I'd brought cable-knit sweaters for her and Susie. My mother had bought them for me. I'd laughed at the time because they were the rustic kind of garment I would never have worn in the city. But here, they were appropriate. One was beige, and the other a lovely ivory, which suited the sisters' creamy complexions better than mine.

The rest of the day stretched on slowly and easily, although half my thoughts were on Brett. The dogs lazed by the fire while Marian taught me how to cook a roast for dinner and bake a pumpkin pie for dessert. She looked shocked when I told her I'd never fashioned a pie crust before.

"We'll fix that," she said. "I'd love to help you become a proficient cook."

Finally, Brett's truck pulled into the driveway. Rex and Piper met him at the door with exuberant barking.

"Where have you been all this time?" Betsy asked him.

"Out and about. If you needed me for anything important, you could have called." He wasn't carrying packages—or even one—meaning he hadn't been Christmas shopping. I'd been hoping . . . well, when would I learn to keep my expectations in check? Why would he buy me a Christmas present after he apologized for one little kiss? Clearly he regretted it.

"Diana has been helping me prepare the meal," Marian said. "In no time at all, she'll know her way around the kitchen like a pro."

"Great," Brett said without enthusiasm. I guessed whatever he had on his mind wasn't me.

Instead of watching football the way everyone in the city did, we played Monopoly for the rest of the afternoon. Each family member already had their favorite piece, which left me with the old-fashioned iron, of all crazy things. I'd never ironed clothes in my life, but I smiled as if elated. Maybe Marian would teach me to iron too. And Betsy promised a quilting lesson. I'd heard there was a fabulous fabric store in Intercourse named Zook's if they had no scraps for this beginner.

I laughed with glee when I landed on Park Place and then foolishly spent too much money to buy what I considered an upscale property. Then I landed in Jail and ran lower on money and property, then landed in Jail again. When had I ever had such rotten luck?

Marian tried to lift my spirits by joking about how it was only a board game, but I felt myself slipping into the doldrums.

"Ordinarily we'd attend a church service on Christmas Eve in the evening," Marian told me, "but Sam thinks the roads might become too hazardous if the temperature drops, as predicted."

"Church?" My family attended church on Easter, and that was so Mom could see what the other women were wearing and scrutinize their hats. "Betsy never mentioned it. I only brought casual clothes."

"Betsy could lend you some if we change our mind, couldn't you, daughter?"

"Absolutely."

"When do you open your Christmas presents?" I tried to change the subject to get both me and Betsy out of the hot seat.

"One present tonight and the rest in the morning," Betsy said.

I considered her statement. "I only have one gift for each of you. When would you like it?"

"Tonight." Betsy grinned. "No delayed gratification for this gal."

"I thought you would say you'd prefer to spread the festivities out as long as you can."

"Not this year. You okay with that?" she asked Susie.

"Sure." Susie rubbed her hands together. "Can't wait."

As we put away the board game, I heard the sound of a large truck making its way to the side of the house.

"What's this all about?" Sam pulled open the drapes.

Brett didn't answer. He grabbed a jacket and stepped out the door.

"What on earth?" Marian said, her nose pressed to a window pane.

"You know as much as I do." Sam peered at the large truck. "I think Brett just told the driver to continue around to the back of the house."

Sam and Marian bundled up and headed outside. Peering out the window, I stayed with Betsy and Susie.

Marian stepped back inside. "Come on, girls. Put on a coat and come see." I felt my gloominess dissipate when I heard her cheery voice. "We found out where Brett spent the day," she said. "He was up near New Holland at a stable, buying a horse."

"A horse?" I couldn't contain my curiosity. I located my jacket and jammed my hands into the sleeves, then followed her.

The trailer's driver and Brett guided a roan-colored mare down the ramp.

"Wait just a minute." Brett dug into his pocket and pulled out a red ribbon, which he tied around the animal's neck. "That's better." He sent me a smile.

"She's lovely," I said.

"Her name is Misty. She's four years old, and the breeder assured me very sweet." Brett led the mare over to me. "Merry Christmas, Diana."

CHAPTER 25

I COULDN'T LOOK AWAY from Brett. "What? I don't understand."

"She's yours." His smile stretched wide. "My Christmas present to you."

"No way. Really?" I turned to the horse. "But where will I keep her?"

"Right here in our barn. We have plenty of room, don't we, Dad?"

"More than enough." Sam slapped his thigh. "You are full of surprises, son. But yes, Diana, we have more than enough space." He spoke to Marian. "Okay with you?"

"Absolutely."

Brett handed me a carrot, which I gave to Misty. She took it from me with soft lips, chomped for a minute, then swallowed. I could tell she was friendly and that I would be able to ride her. I could hardly wait.

"Who knows," Marian said, "you might end up moving to this area."

"Maybe I will." Was I kidding myself?

"Then please persuade our Betsy to move back too."

I laughed. "I'll try. But no guarantees."

I wanted to wrap my arms around Brett and hug him with all my might but decided that would not be appropriate in front of his parents. So I draped my arms around Misty's neck instead and inhaled the heady aroma only a horse can bring. I was transported back to my youth and carefree days at summer camp.

"No 'thank you very much'?" Brett asked, his voice teasing.

"Oh, I'm sorry." I was inundated with emotions. "It's too much," I sputtered. "I can't accept her."

His smile fell. "Is there something wrong with her?"

"No, she's beautiful." I loved her already.

"Well then, why don't you take her down to the barn and see how she does with the other horses?" Sam suggested.

Brett handed me her reins. I led her to the barn and introduced her to the other horses, who seemed interested but not upset.

"I already have a stall ready for her," Brett said. "Next to Honey's." He removed the red ribbon and hung it on a nail. "I'll have to get her a nameplate now that she's an official resident of our house."

"Are you sure your parents don't mind?"

"You saw how they reacted. Pleased as punch."

A couple of hours later, dinner was over. We sat in the living room, sipping hot chocolate, wrapping paper everywhere.

Marian wore the sweater I had given her. I felt somewhat embarrassed as I explained where my gifts had come from, but everyone seemed content and pleased to receive them. Even Brett, who wrapped the scarf around his neck and said he would treasure it because it came from me.

"Hey, Mom, how about dessert?" Betsy said. The two women, followed by Sam and Susie, headed into the kitchen. Only Brett and I remained in the living room, sitting on the floor and leaning against the couch.

"Will you forgive me for surprising you with such an unusual gift?" Brett asked me.

"Of course, if you'll forgive me for not ceasing to think about her. I can't help myself."

"When the snow melts, we'll go out for a ride," he said, "but it may be a few days."

"I told Jesse I wanted to come to their wedding, so I'll be back. Unless for some reason your family is not planning to go."

"Of course I'll go, and you will sit with our family. Next to me." He scooted closer.

"I'd like that. It will be hard for Betsy. Do you think she'll attend the wedding?"

"I would hope so." He paused, then took my hand and brought my fingertips to his lips. "I have another small confession to make."

The voice in my head jumped in to say that he didn't care for me at all and had just given me Misty out of pity. I felt like plugging my ears, but before I could, he pulled me into a tender embrace, his lips and mine meeting tentatively at first and then with passion.

When we parted, he asked, "Do you think you'll be sticking around Lancaster County?"

"Leave before I get a chance to ride Misty?" I couldn't contain a smile. "Highly unlikely."

He was about to say something else when we heard Betsy running down the hall. "There's something wrong. Dad said to put on old jackets and get outside."

CHAPTER 26

PIPER STOOD AT the back door, alternately barking and sniffing the air. I thought I heard wounded animals groaning. No—fire engine sirens. When I opened the door, the pungent odor of smoke drifted in.

Sam bustled out the door behind me, pulling on a wool cap and a second jacket. "Hurry. Jesse's barn is on fire."

I gasped. "No way." What about the animals? What about Midnight?

Through the bare trees, I could make out fire engines already on the property, their headlight beams illuminating smoke billowing out of the barn. I could even see flames spiking from the upper windows.

Piper let out one last bark and then raced off into the darkness. I called her name, but she kept going, heading right for Jesse's farm.

"Brett!" I shouted. It felt like my tongue was moving too slowly, as if my mouth was filled with peanut butter. "Piper's headed to Jesse's place."

Brett took off down the driveway with Betsy sprinting at his heels.

I followed. At the end of the Yoders' driveway, I saw Jesse's sister Cathy directing the fire trucks and a stream of people who appeared out of the darkness—mostly, but not only, Amish men carrying pitchforks and shovels. We followed them toward the inferno.

As I reached the crowd of people in Jesse's barnyard, I saw his sister Nancy, hovering just out of reach of the flames. She was distraught.

"Melvin is in there!"

"Get back!" Jesse shouted, appearing out of nowhere and pulling her out of danger.

"But Melvin!"

Jesse saw me. "Piper just ran into the barn," he said. "I couldn't get to her quickly enough to stop her. Midnight is still in there as well."

"I doubt they can make it out alive," Nancy said, "but they're only animals. What about Melvin?"

Jesse's face grew hard. "Midnight is more than an animal to me." I agreed but was too terrified to speak.

"Jesse," Nancy said. "I love Melvin."

Her proclamation snagged his attention. "What? Why did you never mention anything before?"

"You wouldn't have allowed him to spend so much time over here."

The fire crackled and roared behind us. A bawling cow scurried out, followed by another. Jesse turned. "Are you sure Melvin's in there?"

"*Yah*." She shrank back from the heat.

"And my little dog too?" My voice came out garbled, but she heard me.

"Yah, your *hund* ran in there too."

"I'll get them." Jesse took a deep breath, then charged toward the barn.

"Hey, stop!" A firefighter tried to restrain Jesse. I saw Brett rush over to help him. But Jesse broke free and dashed through the flames and into the barn.

We all fell silent. The firefighters kept working, but the rest of us spectators could only watch as a corner of the barn collapsed. A tunnel of water spewed from one of the trucks, fighting the flames at the entrance of the barn, creating a tunnel for Jesse to come back through. I couldn't imagine how he or Piper could escape death's jaws. I felt faint, then nauseous.

Minutes later—it felt like hours—I saw Piper racing through the door. Jesse staggered out behind her, covered with soot and carrying a man on his back. The paramedics rushed over to attend to them.

"Melvin," Nancy whispered, tears seeping from her eyes. We hurried over to them.

"Is he alive?" I asked the medic, looking at the unconscious young man.

"He's breathing." The medic had already placed an oxygen mask over Melvin's blackened face.

Piper licked Jesse's hand, and he looked to me. "Your dog showed me where Melvin was. A rafter had fallen on him, pinned him down."

I scooped my darling Piper off the ground and clasped her tightly. "What would I do without you?"

"She's one brave little dog," Brett said.

I should thank him for the compliment, but I was too shaken up to respond. There was still no sign of Midnight. I pictured him panicking and galloping back into the barn, where gluttonous flames consumed him. I hoped Jesse wouldn't be alone tomorrow when he found the lifeless animal.

I felt the wind shift and heard a man shout, "Save the house!" The voice sounded familiar. I turned to see that it was Bishop Harold. He was looking up to where a plume of sooty smoke moved toward Jesse's home, bringing with it sparks of burning hay.

Brett must have noticed my expression. "Many of the fireman are volunteers, including an occasional bishop." Then he loped back to the barn to help.

One of the groups of firefighters shifted their hose, spraying the roof of the house with a deluge of water. They were so much braver than I was. Erratic thoughts zigzagged through my head. I felt vulnerable, yet thankful.

I stood for an hour watching the chaos until I was sure the house was safe and the barn was smoldering—the fire contained.

Marian placed a hand on my shoulder, making me start. "There's nothing more we can do here," she said. "Want to walk back to the house together? I need to check my turkey."

I realized I was trembling. "Okay, thanks." My voice quivered. "In a minute."

A single siren blared as the ambulance pulled away from the barnyard, taking Melvin to the hospital.

"If it weren't for Jesse and Piper, Melvin would be dead," Marian said.

I relished Piper's weight in my arms and hugged her.

As Marian slipped her arm around my waist, I looked over my shoulder at the mayhem. This certainly wasn't what I expected to see in Amish country on Christmas Eve.

Marian let out a puff of air. "I can't imagine the mess Jesse and his sisters will wake up to tomorrow."

"If they get any sleep at all tonight." I shook my head.

The sky was draining of color. "The weather report predicts a warming trend tomorrow," she said, "but I assume all that water the firemen sprayed will freeze."

Feeling dizzy, I wanted to be back in the city where I recognized the sounds and knew which corner I was standing on.

CHAPTER 27

THIRTY MINUTES LATER, after a shower to remove the stench of smoke from my skin and my hair, I dressed and then stood at the bedroom window with Piper by my side, staring at the glowing remains of the barn through the trees. A cloak of sadness hindered my movements. I finally forced myself into bed but slept no more than a few hours. Still, the next morning I came downstairs to find an empty house, save the two dogs.

Freshly baked muffins, butter, and honey sat on the table. One plate. And a note from Marian stating she expected me to eat as many as I wanted and to make myself at home in the kitchen.

I thought about Misty. In spite of last night's tragedy, I owned a lovely horse, and I wanted to see her. After eating, I layered up, pilfered a carrot from the refrigerator, and jammed it in a pocket of one of Betsy's work coats.

When I stepped outside, I found the air warmer, probably above freezing. It wasn't spring yet, but I was gratified for these peekaboo warm windows before the temperature turned around and plunged back to winter.

With Piper at my side, I wandered to the barn to find Misty, who I'm sure recognized me. She and Piper seemed to be fine together. The horse had settled in well. Someone, probably Brett or Sam, had already fed her. I would thank him later.

I gathered my fortitude and set out for what was once Jesse's barn.

As I ambled up the driveway, I was amazed to smell brewing coffee. Piper and I followed the scent. In Jesse's barnyard, I found a group of Amish women behind fold-up card tables filled with coffee, bottled water, some kind of egg dish, and cinnamon rolls. I was blown away by the generosity of the Amish community.

Betsy approached me. "Good morning, girlfriend," she said as she gave me a quick hug. "And merry Christmas."

"Merry Christmas to you."

"Looks like we'll have to put off the festivities for a while," she said. "At least until tonight or tomorrow."

Betsy noticed my gaze moving through the dozens of men who were working to remove debris from the charred base of the barn.

"Brett drove Jesse and Nancy to the hospital to check on Melvin," she said. "I don't know which one was more upset."

"What?" I hesitated to ask. "Did Jesse find Midnight?"

"No, never mind." She smooshed her lips together. "Hey, you're in for a big treat once the men start rebuilding the barn."

"I've seen photographs—"

"Well, they won't compare to the real thing, once this area is cleared and the lumber arrives." Her words burbled out. "Believe me, you have never seen anything like a barn raising."

"Too bad a barn had to burn down first," I said in an attempt at levity that fell flat.

"Too bad a lot of things happened," Betsy said. I assumed she was referring to Jesse and Naomi, but I said nothing.

She stepped across an icy patch of the yard with care. "I overheard the foreman say it will take several days to clear the area out enough to start rebuilding."

"A real foreman? Where did he come from?"

"The Amish man with the most experience takes charge of construction like this."

A draft horse dragged a charred chunk of timber through a muddy puddle and out of what used to be the barn. The man leading the horse continued on to a pile of charred timber I assumed would be burned.

"The bearded Amish men are married," Betsy told me. "If they're clean shaven, it means they're single."

I wondered what Brett would do during the barn raising, if anything. Were non-Amish men even allowed to take part in such a production? I couldn't imagine Brett standing around doing nothing, watching others labor.

Men took breaks from their work and meandered over to collect coffee, bottled water, and the gooey-looking cinnamon rolls. I noticed one of the women serving was Naomi, as beautiful as ever in a teal dress and black coat. I also noticed the line at her table was the longest. She flirted and smiled at one young man in particular, who wore jeans and a baseball hat. The man lingered to chat until Bishop Harold marched over and stood near them with his arms folded. The young man noticed him and turned, shrinking back to a group of men his age and younger.

"Naomi sure is, uh, vivacious," I said.

"Don't get me started."

I decided to steer our subject in another direction. "Who's the guy in the baseball cap?"

"Tommy. He's Amish but doesn't attend church or follow the Ordnung."

"Has he been shunned?"

"No," she said. "He's Amish but was never baptized. The bishop, the ministers, and the deacon—the whole congregation—would forgive him if he returned to the fold and confessed his sins."

"That's amazing."

The corners of Betsy's mouth lifted, but her eyes remained sad. "The Amish are quick to forgive. And yes, you're right, they are amazing."

"What's he doing here today?"

"Many men come when their neighbors need them. Community is important to them, being part of a team. They get to see their friends. And they love every aspect of barn raisings. I guess it's like how the Amish women adore work frolics, quilting, or gardening together."

I was happy to be part of this community even if I really wasn't. I didn't have this in New York. Sure, I knew a few neighbors, joked with the guy at the deli, and greeted Carlos the doorman, but our relationships were superficial. Betsy was my only real friend.

"Am I allowed to have a cinnamon roll?" My mouth salivated.

"Sure, when the workers are finished. Help out with the serving lines and nab one."

I carried a plastic garbage bag around and collected empty water bottles and paper plates. Several people told me "*denke*," which I took to mean thank you. I smiled and decided I needed to learn how to say "you're welcome" properly.

Once the line to the tables dwindled, I helped myself to what may have been the best melt-in-your-mouth cinnamon roll ever. These weren't purchased from a grocery store, for sure. I envisioned a woman staying up all night to prepare it. The Amish were awesome.

I stuck around to help however I could. Brett returned with Jesse and Nancy a couple hours later. They'd waited until Merlin was released from the hospital. He'd been instructed to rest. Brett dropped him off at his family's home. Nancy looked crestfallen when she told me that Merlin must not have visitors for a few days, but I was elated to hear the doctor had pronounced there was no permanent damage to his lungs and only superficial burns. When I asked Jesse about his own health, he shrugged. "I don't have time to be sick. I'm certainly not going to rest when I have a barn to build."

"But Jesse," Betsy said, "one day's rest on Christmas won't make much difference. Not with this much of a mess to contend with."

"If I have extra time today, I will be looking for Midnight to see if he made it out alive."

The word *miracle* came to mind, because that's what it would take.

"No one has found Midnight's body yet," Betsy said, "but I've heard of horses refusing to leave burning barns and returning to their stalls, where they perished."

"Poor creatures." I shuddered to think of Piper or Misty in a blazing barn. And I was thankful.

CHAPTER 28

I COULD SCARCELY BELIEVE Christmas night was approaching. I was curious how my parents were doing but didn't want to disturb them with a call. I hoped they were together, ordering their Chinese food as planned. I envisioned Mom wearing her sparkly new earrings—all dolled up and fussing over my father. Being her most charming self.

As the sun set, the work demolishing the barn ground to a halt, and the many exhausted people dispersed. I recalled my brave little Piper running into the blazing barn. How did she know a man was trapped inside? Maybe she heard Melvin's calling for help above the hubbub. Living in the city, she'd heard many sirens. I wished she could tell me. No matter, she deserved a canine purple heart, if there were such a thing. Over the years I had heard of many heroic deeds dogs had performed. Now I had proof positive.

The Yoder family straggled home, washed up, and gathered around the dinner table. Marian had prepared a stuffed turkey, sweet potatoes, green beans, and corn muffins. I enjoyed each mouthful. And sitting next to Brett, who had saved me a spot.

"The work can wait," Sam said. "This evening, we will be grateful for our blessings and celebrate the birth of our Savior."

After we ate, we gathered around the tree with mugs of hot cider to open gifts. We were all tired, but no one wanted to turn in early.

"Diana has already received a gift, right?" Betsy chuckled. "But Misty wouldn't be happy in here."

"Oh dear," I said, "should I look in on her?"

"It's all taken care of," Brett said, glancing into my face.

"She's blanketed and fed?" I had a lot to learn.

"Taken care of." Brett smiled at me.

Sam and Marian gave Brett, Betsy, and me each a small gift—all books. Mine was on the care of horses. How did they know I needed it? This seemed to be a conspiracy of the best kind. Betsy received a novel by Elin Hildebrand, and Brett a memoir by Ira Wagler, which they both seemed happy to receive. "I know this ex-Amish guy and have been meaning to read his memoir," Brett said.

Susie unwrapped her present to find a collection of hardbound books. "Novels by the Brontë Sisters," she said. I loved reading but was surprised by her excitement.

"Haven't you read all of those already?" Betsy asked her.

"Not all of them. And the books I read were borrowed from the library. These will be mine."

"Can I borrow one from you?" Betsy said in jest.

"Not if you're going to take it to New York City."

It occurred to me that I hadn't heard a TV since I'd arrived, just mellow music in the background playing a medley of Christmas carols. "Sing choirs of angels . . ." I felt my lids slide closed, and my head droop. Sam's voice woke me; I jerked my head back upright.

"Want to call it a night?" he asked me.

"Sorry." I covered my yawn. "I can't recall the last time I just nodded off."

"It's all this fresh Lancaster County air my parents will tell you." Betsy skimmed through my book, then handed it to me. "This looks good," she said.

"You may go upstairs, dear," Marian said. "We've all had a busy day."

"Thanks, I think I will. I'm exhausted." I plodded up the stairs, but delayed getting undressed. I sat on the bed and opened my new book. Every page opened up to something interesting. I could hardly wait to try out my new skills on Misty. I wondered when the weather would be warm enough to attempt riding her. Then a ghastly thought entered my mind. I needed a saddle. I had never learned to ride bareback. Now what? I decided to ask Betsy her opinion, but when I knocked on her door, she didn't answer.

I heard voices chatting on the first floor. Apparently the Yoders hadn't turned in. Perhaps they were opening more presents in my absence. Fair enough.

I heard Brett was talking to someone on the phone. As I got closer, I realized he was arguing more than conversing.

"Please, not tonight," Brett said. "Doesn't everyone in the county know that Midnight is missing? Someone will spot him and contact you." Brett sighed. "Okay, I'll be around to pick you up in an hour."

"The road could be a sheet of ice," Sam said. "Can't this wait till tomorrow morning?" "What about Jesse's sisters?" Marian asked. "He's being selfish to leave them by themselves on Christmas."

Sam glanced at his wife. "I don't know if I'd go that far, but I do think Brett is acting foolhardy."

"Hey, big brother, how about if I come along with you?" Betsy said. "Maybe we can look in on Melvin."

"Melvin's family lives way in Leola." Brett's voice turned gruff. "I'm not driving that far."

"You owe him," Betsy said.

Brett sounded tired. "No need to tell me what I already know. When will my debt be paid, Betsy? Never?"

As I stepped into the room, I saw Brett massaging the bridge of his nose.

Sam answered before his daughter could. "Jesse and his father granted you forgiveness before you even asked them. To withhold it would be a sin for them."

What was all this talk of sin and forgiveness? I thought about the queen of the cliques when I was in high school. I'd doubt I'd recognize her of I bumped into her in Bloomingdale's today, but I had no intention of forgiving her for excluding me or stealing away any guy I looked at twice. Those experiences had wounded me to my core. Was Sam saying that not forgiving her was a sin? Should I follow her on Facebook or Instagram?

I sat on the couch between Marian and Betsy. Piper curled at my feet, giving me the feeling of security. I reach down and stroked her until she flopped on her side and reveled in my fingers' touch. I would never let her out on a night like tonight, let alone go out myself.

"There's no way around it." Brett stood. "The faster I get this over with, the sooner I'll be home again."

"Son, Jesse's taking advantage of your kind heart," Marian said.

"Wouldn't you help out a friend, especially on Christmas?" Brett turned to Sam. "Dad, I know you would."

"Yes, I suppose I would." He looked Brett in the eye. "Please be careful, son."

"I will."

I envisioned Brett's pickup hitting black ice, skidding off the road and plowing into a tree. I tried to erase the image from my mind but felt as if I were sinking in quicksand. Would I lose the love of my life? Should I run after him and tell him I adored him? No, I was still unsure. I didn't trust my conflicting emotions.

CHAPTER 29

WAITING FOR BRETT'S return, I tried to relax and appear carefree with the Yoders in the living room for a couple of hours. After what seemed like forever, we heard his truck in the driveway. Betsy and Marian hurried after Piper and Rex to meet him at the kitchen door. Not wanting to appear too anxious, I followed after them but lagged back.

Brett stepped out of his snowy boots and into suede slippers. "We covered every inch of the county and asked everyone we met, but no one has seen Midnight. Or will admit it, anyway. There's always a possibility someone stole him. But at least I did my best."

"I'll bet Jesse was grateful," Marian said.

"It's hard to tell. And does it really matter?"

"No, you did the right thing." Marian produced a lopsided smile. "I'm glad to have you home again. Safe and sound."

So was I, but I didn't say anything out loud.

"Jesse told me that the fire marshal came over this afternoon and told him he thinks the barn fire was a case of arson," Brett said. "Apparently other than lightning most barn fires are caused by arsonists."

"Who and why?" I leaned forward, shocked. "He should've had Piper there to warn him that someone was on the property."

"Most farmers do have a dog," Sam said.

"Jesse's old mutt died last year," Brett said. "He needs a new one."

"Or an alarm system," I said.

"Not possible without electricity." Betsy explained the obvious.

"Oh, yeah." I gazed at the Christmas tree lights and pondered what living without electricity would be like. The Amish seemed to manage fine, at least with the help of their neighbors. I recalled all the people who showed up last night, carrying shovels and pitchforks. But I also now thought about someone who would intentionally set Jesse's barn on fire.

I considered possible suspects. "How about that guy named Tommy? Could he be a pyromaniac?"

"He's rough around the edges, but we must not judge a book by its cover," Sam said.

"You're right." But Tommy was still at the top of my list, after the way he flirted with Naomi in front of her parents and the whole crowd. But what did I know? Jesse could have enemies from anywhere. Jealousy could do that.

Marian yawned, and Sam chuckled. "It looks like we're all ready to turn in."

"Do you need help cleaning the kitchen?" I asked Marian.

"It can wait until tomorrow."

"Should we fix food and bring it to Jesse's house tomorrow?" Betsy turned to me. "The Amish celebrate Second Christmas, which includes friends and neighbors."

"I assume Naomi's family will help him and his sisters." Sam stoked the fire. "Not to mention his aunts and uncles and cousins. He has plenty of family and friends."

"And what's wrong with that?" Her face red and angry, Betsy clasped her hands around her slim waist. "Since when did you become so judgmental?"

In a flash, Sam's temper ignited. He looked ready to explode. "What is wrong with you, young lady?"

Betsy burst into sobs. "You two have never loved me. Brett has always been your favorite, then Susie."

Susie shrank back. Not that I blamed her. Suddenly this picture-perfect family reminded me of my own, which in a strange way gave me comfort.

"Where did this resentment come from?" Marian asked. "We love you all very much. Equally."

"Don't make me laugh. Brett has always been number one around here. Then precious, little Susie arrived."

Her mother's jaw dropped open. "How long have you felt this way?"

"Since . . . since you wouldn't let me go to college."

"Wouldn't let you?" Sam's voice revealed astonishment. "We begged you to attend college or community college, but you refused. You chose to move to New York City instead. We could see no point in it but didn't try to stop you."

"Because you were glad to see me leave."

"Not true." Marian's right hand covered her heart. "We were trying to let you grow into a responsible adult."

"We accepted your decision, even if we didn't like it," Sam said.

"You left without even saying goodbye." Brett got in Betsy's face. "Mom moped around the house for weeks. You owe her an apology."

"Yeah, an apology," Susie echoed. "I came home from school, and you were gone."

Betsy didn't respond but instead burst into tears and dashed upstairs to her room. A few quiet minutes later, the rest of us toddled off to bed, as well. What on earth had happened?

CHAPTER 30

PIPER WOKE ME in the morning. "Too early, girl," I said, but she persisted in whimpering. I glanced out the window and noticed the sky was light already. I was blown away that I'd slept so well after the Yoder family's dispute last night. Who would have thought it? They weren't the perfect family after all. I guessed all families had their problems.

Someone tapped on my door. I put on my bathrobe and cracked the door enough for Piper to dart out and head down the stairs.

"Please let me in," Betsy said. "I'm so embarrassed." She pushed the door open. I backstepped into the room. "I was sent up here on a mission to bring you downstairs with me."

"But I just woke up. I'm only half awake. I need to shower and get dressed first."

"Okay, I'll give you fifteen minutes. Then, please, do come downstairs. I feel awful for what you had to listen to. We all do. I don't think I've ever behaved so poorly."

I hurried through my shower and combed my hair. No matter what I'd seen, I was Betsy's guest and needed to behave that way.

Piper waited for me at the bottom of the stairs and led me into the living room, where I saw the rest of the family gathered. The conversation stopped as soon as I came in. Sam stood.

"As head of the family, it's my responsibility to tell you how very sorry we acted so abominably last night. On Christmas, no less. I could make up excuses, but they would not take back our snarly dispute."

"Not a problem. Really." My mind replayed their conversation. "My family isn't without its faults." The tongue was indeed the most wicked part of the body, full of deadly poison. Oh dear, I was starting to think the way the Mennonites did, quoting from the Bible—as best I could. But it was the truth. I'd seen in my own family how the tongue could cut into a person like a sword.

Marian moved over and gave me a lovely hug. "I echo everything Sam said. You must think we're a bunch of—well, I can't even imagine what you think of us. Really, I hope we didn't ruin your Christmas."

"We all apologize," Brett said and tussled Betsy's hair. "Will you forgive us?"

I felt swathed in warmth. "Nothing to forgive. It's just a slice of family life where I live."

Brett spoke in a soft voice. "A question, Diana. Are you ready for coffee, or shall you open a present first?"

Confused, I looked at him. There were no gifts left under the tree. "We opened all of the presents last night," I said.

"Don't I see one more under the tree, way in the back?" Sam stood up to inspect it and read the card. "For Diana."

"Oh no, I can't accept another gift." I felt tears pricking at the backs of my eyes. "Not after I have been welcomed into this family. Not to mention Misty." I turned to face Brett. "I still can't thank you enough."

Sam got to his feet and brought me a large clumsy package that had been obscured by the tree. I couldn't imagine what it was. "This is from all of us," he said. His face was kind, almost as if he were my own father on a good day.

I put my arms out to take it, but he kept hold of the item. "This might be a bit heavy for you at first."

I felt as if I were the center of a giant surprise birthday party. The whole family was smiling at me. Even Piper wagged her tail and watched.

Sam hoisted the package on the coffee table. I could see by the way he handled the parcel that it was indeed heavy.

"Go ahead and open it," he said. "It won't bite, and it will sure make riding a lot easier for you."

I pulled off the paper. "A saddle? Exactly what I need." I was overcome by their generously.

CHAPTER 31

"I CAN'T ACCEPT THIS. It's too much."
How would I ever pay them back?

"Think of it as a gift to Misty," Brett said.

"It's a Second Christmas present from all of us," Betsy assured me.

"You can't say no," Brett said.

My heart swelled with gladness as my hands explored the mahogany-brown leather. I could hardly wait to see how it fit Misty.

Brett must have anticipated my thoughts. "While Mom's making breakfast, let's take this out to the barn and see if Misty likes it."

I could see Sam restraining Susie. "You stay here and help with breakfast," he said. "There will be plenty of time to see Misty."

"Why is it Brett gets to have all the fun?" she whined.

"Let's not have a replay of last night, okay?"

As I followed Brett to the barn, I thought about splendid Manhattan, all decked out in finery. I decided I liked this way of life better. Who would have thought? Of course, my change of mindset had a lot to do with the man carrying my new saddle.

The air felt warmer than yesterday, and the sky a hazy blue.

"Hey, Misty, what do you think of this?" Brett asked my horse as he approached her stall. She was already blanketed and ready as Brett put the saddle over her. It fit perfectly. He admitted he'd already tried it on her to make sure.

I was still awestruck. Piper danced at my feet, but Misty didn't seem to mind. Her ears stood up, and her eyes were soft. She nickered. This mare was perfect, as far as I could tell. I couldn't wait to ride her.

"Merry Christmas," I told her. I felt swathed in warmth.

"How about me?" Brett asked. "Do I get a Merry Christmas too?" He extracted a small sprig of mistletoe out of his pocket and put it over his head. I drew closer, glad for the invitation to kiss him. But outside, a bell clanged.

"Breakfast is ready," Marian called. "Come and get it."

"Okay," Brett yelled. "In a minute." Then he lowered his volume and said, "Hey, Diana, where's my kiss?" Before I could answer, his lips were brushing mine, then softening—sending a thrill through me. I was famished but would have gladly stayed in the barn with him necking, as my mother would call it.

I hated the kiss to end but said, "We'd better go." I was glad I hadn't applied lipstick; he'd be wearing it. I figured my cheeks were flushed—a healthy glow.

I gave Misty's sturdy neck one last stroke and then followed Brett to the house. He gave the barn a looking-over before he closed the door securely. An eerie feeling invaded me when I considered how easily a person could enter this barn. The chaotic scene next door still nattered in my brain.

Marian had prepared an elaborate meal for us, much to my delight. It seemed skinny jeans would be out of the picture if I didn't do something to curb my appetite.

We spent another long, lazy day playing board games and laughing by the fire. The snow was melting quickly, but Sam forbade Brett from going out to look for Midnight again. "Someone has found the horse by now, if he's out there to be found."

THE NEXT DAY the temperature was still warm; the snow kept melting.

Betsy and I wandered over to Jesse's and watched men remove more rubble. Despite the sun, I was glad for my borrowed hat and rubber boots. They felt like mine, anyway. With so many by the back door, Betsy said no one would miss a pair if I kept them.

One day ran into the next. Neither Betsy or I said anything about going back to New York. Each day I helped the women pour coffee and serve bottled water, then clean up after everyone ate. The Yoders continued to treat me like an honored guest, and I enjoyed Brett's attention. The only dark spot was that Midnight had not been found.

One afternoon, the easy routine was interrupted by the rumble of truck engines approaching the worksite. I could tell by the men's expressions that something exciting was about to happen long before the first of three trucks carrying lumber pulled into the barnyard. Jesse seemed beside himself with euphoria as he and Brett inspected the timber and found it blemish free. I heard Jesse thank Brett, who had used his company's connections to arrange for a discount.

The foreman told the drivers where to park and which truck to unload first. The fragrant aroma of freshly milled timber was new to me. I loved it.

The men worked as an orchestrated team, as if they had done this together many times. They pounded nails into two-by-fours, placed huge support beams into place, and erected the skeleton of what would be a barn even bigger than the original.

I admired Brett's dexterity and skill as he worked alongside the Amish men. I also couldn't help but admire the sculpted muscles I could see through his T-shirt and his easygoing personality as he talked with his fellow workers in English and Pennsylvania Dutch.

As the day progressed, I watched men construct walls on the ground, then, working together, lift them into place. There must have been a hundred men there. I understood why the group needed a foreman, a man of maturity and wisdom, to orchestrate the project. Several times the bearded man yelled at Jesse, who insisted on climbing ladders to the highest points, with Tommy on his heels.

I looked around at one point and saw Naomi eying them both. Was she comparing them and deciding which one she wished to marry, even with her father standing close by?

At one point, Jesse and Tommy bumped into each other. With twisted faces, they both whirled around and looked ready to throw a punch. The barnyard fell silent until the bishop approached.

"I don't care whose barn this is, no shenanigans. Get back to work."

Jesse took a deep breath and nodded. Then, casually, he extracted a handkerchief from his pocket and dried his brow. I wondered if the fabric had been a present from Naomi, because I spotted the letter *N* embroidered on the corner. With a smirk, Jesse returned it to his pocket and scuttled up another ladder.

Tommy walked away, brazenly approaching Naomi and speaking loud enough for me to hear. "I could take you out to dinner later and give you a ride home after. You know, I have a car." He leaned toward her, but she inched back, glancing at her father. Did she really love this guy?

After a few hours, the relentless pounding of nails ended, and the crew came together for the noontime meal. I was learning the jargon.

"Anything I can do for you, Diana?" I glanced over and saw Brett headed my way. "Want to walk back with me for lunch at our house?"

I had no business being hungry again, but I was. Apparently, watching those men laboring for hours while eating two cinnamon rolls had made me ravenous.

"I should help serve up food at one of the tables." I enjoyed the interaction with the Amish.

"Or we could stop on the way and visit Misty. I told Mom we might."

I appreciated his thoughtfulness. I hadn't spent much time with Misty, though she was always on my mind. "Yes, I'd love seeing her. Of course."

And I wanted to spend time alone with Brett. But when we reached the barn, we found Sam checking for frozen pipes. "In spite of all my precautions, one of these is frozen," he said. "Think I'll use the wait-and-see method."

I visited Misty for a few lovely minutes, then heard Marian ringing the bell for us to come to the house.

Betsy poked her head in. "Hi, everyone. Lunch is ready." She sent Brett and me a smirk. "Coming?"

CHAPTER 32

GOOD NEWS ABOUNDED—DEPENDING who you were. Over the table, we discussed how an Amish man had managed to lasso Midnight and had kept the stallion in his barn until he could get word to Jesse, who was ecstatic. Jesse had offered an award, but the fellow refused it. "Nothing I wouldn't do for any other man," the Amishman said.

The conversation shifted to Jesse's approaching marriage. No date had been set. When Betsy started to sulk, Brett declared that she could find someone better. "His wife will spend a lifetime being his babysitter."

"How dare you say that when you're the one who killed his mother?"

Brett sat back as if she'd slapped him in the face.

"Please, I beg of you," Marian said, wringing her hands together, "no more bickering. Do you want to scare Diana away from here forever?"

Brett and Betsy exchanged quick glances. "No," they both said.

"In fact," Brett said, "I'm hoping she'll stay in Lancaster County."

"Hey," Betsy said, "you took the words right out of my mouth. I've been thinking that Diana and I can rent a little cottage in the area, or an apartment, if Misty can stay here." She swiveled to face me. "How about it?"

I'd been pondering that scenario myself but hadn't come to a conclusion. I mean, could I really leave Manhattan, the Big Apple, and everything I loved? Or thought I loved? I wondered if everything I loved was actually here.

Marian stepped into save me. "Perhaps this is not the time or place for Diana to make a decision that will change her life. Give her time to think it over." She turned to Betsy. "How and where will you earn a living?"

"Pretty much doing what I'm doing now. I'll stop in Zook's Fabric Store in Intercourse to see if they need a salesperson. Not everyone working there is Amish."

"Sounds like a splendid idea, honey. I can't get enough of that place."

Brett's phone rang; he stood and stepped away to talk. When he came back, he told us, "Just Jesse calling me back to say everything is on track. Midnight's safe and sound, and Jesse has found a way to transport him home." Brett stashed his phone. "Jesse should get rid of that animal, but no use arguing with him. I told him I'd help out if he needs it. Give him a ride to the area."

"I want to go too," Betsy said. "Please, please, please, take me with you."

"And how will you help him?" Marian asked.

"You never know what a second set of hands can do. You've always said I have a good way with horses. The poor animal is probably mixed up, what with his barn gone."

Sam shook his head. "It's not the only thing that's mixed up."

"Well . . . I don't want to be left behind."

Sam narrowed his eyes at her. "Betsy . . ."

"Okay, Dad, I get the picture."

"I'll miss all the excitement," I said, "but I need to go back to the city to pick up some more clothes if I'm going to be staying in the area for a while." I smiled at Betsy. "Meanwhile, maybe you can find us a place to live."

"Yay, living with a girlfriend will be fun," Betsy said. "I have a place in mind already. You can count on me."

I hoped I was making the right decision. What would I do if she couldn't find a place for us? Or if I couldn't find a job?

Brett said, "I'll drive you to the city, Diana."

"Are you sure that's not too much trouble? The traffic can be so hectic, and the snow probably hasn't melted entirely."

"Maybe you should hire a driver," Marian said. "Sam has a cousin who does it for a living. It would be our gift to you."

"Oh no, I could not accept another gift from you. But thanks for your generosity. In fact, I'd love to hire him."

"The 'him' is actually a woman. She's very capable and has a four-wheel-drive vehicle."

It made sense, but I'd really hoped that Brett would insist; we'd get a chance to spend extra time together. What a mistake I'd made to turn him down.

"Has she ever navigated heavy traffic?" I asked.

"I'm sure she can handle it. She takes folks down to the Philadelphia airport, Newark, and to JFK."

"Then that sounds great." I shrugged off my disappointment.

Sam called his cousin and made the arrangements. Judy had the next couple of days free, and she said she would love to visit a niece in New York. The traffic wouldn't be a problem, especially if there weren't planes to catch. She would drop me off at my apartment and pick me up the next day. Or in two days, if that would be more convenient. She wouldn't mind taking in a show or musical.

CHAPTER 33

THE NEXT MORNING, I bid farewell to Brett and Betsy. I felt a little glum when Brett didn't say he'd miss me, but at least Betsy was in good spirits.

I threw the essentials in my overnight bag and lugged it to the bottom of the stairs, where Piper lay sleeping. Her eyes cracked open for a moment before she rolled onto her side and fell asleep again.

"Hurry up, girlie, you're coming with me." But I'd turned invisible. Was she pretending to be sleeping? Payback time for my getting a horse and splitting my attention?

A vehicle honked outside. "Judy's out front," Sam said, looking out the window.

"Piper won't come with me," I told him. My own dog was deserting me. "Do you mind if I leave her here? I'll be back tomorrow, or the next day at the latest."

"Not at all. She fits right in."

He was right; we both fit in. Did I really even want to go back to the city? I needed to gather more of my clothes, but I also wanted some space to reexamine my feelings for Brett. Was he marriage material? I adored his parents, but they would be my in-laws, not my happily ever after. If there was such a thing.

Judy was a tall and buxom woman with a wide smile. She wore a longish wool coat over her dress and looked capable of dealing with any situation. I liked her immediately and chose to sit in the front seat with her. "I'll be able to give you better directions and also enjoy the view."

Most of the snow had melted from the city streets by the time we got to Manhattan, but mountains of gray still stood against the curbs. Horns honked as we stopped at a light, and I pointed out the window. "It's that building right over there."

"Do you mind if I just let you off?" Judy asked.

"That's fine. I have your number to arrange the trip back." I scrambled to get out of her vehicle with my overnight bag before the light turned green.

I expected one of our doormen to come and assist me with the door, but no one did. As I walked into the lobby, a man got up from the desk and wandered toward me at a leisurely pace.

"Who are you?" I asked. I wasn't going to hand a stranger my suitcase or anything else.

He folded his arms across his chest. "I could ask you the same thing."

I attempted to walk past him to the elevator. "I live here."

He barred my way. "Live where?"

"Where's Carlos?" I asked. "What's going on?"

"He's on vacation to visit his sick mother."

I hated to admit it, but I'd never even considered that our doorman had a mother. "Are my parents at home?" I asked him.

"And who exactly are your parents?"

Right, he didn't know me. "The Manzellas. Seventh floor."

"Got proof of that?"

"If only Carlos was here." I reached into my purse, fished around, and realized my wallet must still be sitting on my dresser in Lancaster County. "I don't have my ID with me, but I've lived here for most of my life." Anyone from the building would recognize me, but the lobby was empty.

I fished in my purse further and felt something cool and metal. A key.

I turned on my most hostile New York City voice and hoped he'd buy it. "Look, I've got the key to my apartment. This is where I live. Let me in right this minute before I call the building's supervisor."

"Okay, okay, don't get all huffy." He scratched his jaw. "Manzella, huh? They left for the Caribbean yesterday."

"Without telling me?" I hadn't meant to speak my musings out loud.

"I heard the words *second honeymoon*," he said with a wink.

Well, it was better than coming home to find that the reunion hadn't lasted and they'd filed for divorce. But why hadn't they told me?

"Are you Diana?" he asked. I was so perturbed I nodded without answering.

"In that case, it won't hurt to tell you that a huge bouquet of flowers showed up a couple hours ago with your name on it. Real beauties. I had them sent upstairs."

I thought about Brett. Had he ordered me flowers? What a sweetheart.

I rode the elevator to our floor and couldn't get the door open fast enough. Inside, on an end table, stood a stupendous floral arrangement of long-stem roses, hydrangeas, orchids, and exotic blooms I'd never seen before. The luxurious flowers stopped me in my tracks. I tore open the card with my name on it, only to see a note not from Brett, but from

Vince. He said he'd made a terrible mistake. I was the woman he loved.

Wasn't he married? How had he already divorced the woman he'd dropped me for? Or was he cheating on her? He was the last person on earth I wanted to see during my final days in New York. Was this some kind of sick joke?

My cell phone rang; I recognized Vince's number. I would not answer. I simply would not recognize him as a human being. But curiosity got the better of me. "Hello, Vince," I said in monotone, as if I'd been expecting his call.

"Hey, baby. Like the flowers?"

All I felt like doing was screaming. Maybe I should. Or maybe I should just hang up. As I pondered my options, he said, "I can't make it without you, Diana. I've been such a fool."

"Aren't you married now? What do you want from me? To fool around on the side?" I was embarrassed to think how many tears I'd shed over this creep.

"I'm still single." He sounded pathetic, like he wanted me to feel sorry for him after all he'd put me through. I pictured him raking his fingers through his wavy, black hair. He was physically attractive, I had to admit. "Candy took up with some rich Wall Street dude and called off the wedding." He paused for a moment, then let out a sob. Was it real? "I don't blame you if you hate me for the rest of your life. I was a thoughtless jerk." He sniffed, then sneezed.

A sound like white noise filled my ears. He had no right to ask anything of me. I hated him.

"Well, do you like the flowers?" he asked. "They cost me a bundle."

"Yes, they're very nice, but not necessary." If I had an ounce of dignity I would hang up on him this moment. I wanted to call him a lousy scoundrel but held my tongue. Pathetic as it was, I also wanted to ask him why he'd dumped me. There had to be something wrong with me.

"Hey, babe, I have an idea," he said. "How about you and I go out to dinner tonight?"

In the back of my mind, I heard an Amishman talking about forgiveness, the way Jesse's father had forgiven Brett. But surely that didn't mean rolling over in front of a semitruck and playing dead.

Vince was still jabbering. "I'll pick you up. We could go out to the most expensive, snazziest restaurant in town. Per Se, if French food suits your fancy. Or Italian is always good. I'll pay for everything, even the finest champagne." His voice turned seductive. "Where would you like to go?"

Anywhere? I admonished myself for even thinking about which upscale place I'd like to eat at tonight. But not with Vince. Did I even want to dine at swanky restaurants anymore? No, I longed for the simplicity of Lancaster County.

"A steak as only New York can make it, or Maine lobster?"

I was hungry, and the thought made my mouth water.

"No, I don't want you coming here."

"Then how about I meet you in that little Italian place around the corner?"

I could smell the melting cheese and the lasagna, tempting me when I knew my refrigerator was empty.

"We could enjoy your favorites, no strings attached," he said.

I felt myself beginning to cave.

"So, you're as free as a bird?" I said, trying to find out the shoddy details.

"What could I do? She was having an affair. She called me a loser. Me, of all people."

"Maybe you two will get back together again." I glanced at the exquisite flowers.

"Nah, she and I are through. That's how we both want it." He hesitated for a minute. "I ran into your father at the club a couple days ago. He said you've been in Lancaster County and love it. If you like the area, I could buy us a place."

"There is no us."

"But admit it. We had good times." He paused. "You like it there with those horses and buggies? I'll buy us some acreage with a barn. Build you any kind of house unless we find one to your liking. I saw an ad for a small farm yesterday. Five acres. You see, I've been thinking of you."

I hate to admit I was flattered but I reminded myself he was a scumbag.

"Will you at least give it some thought, baby?"

"I have a new horse." Where did that come from? I should seal my mouth closed with duct tape.

"Cool," he said. "Where do you keep it?"

CHAPTER 34

I CHIDED MYSELF AS I savored the antipasto
misto in the cozy Italian restaurant a block from
our apartment building. The smell of warm cheese
wove through the room. Accordion music from the
sound system and laughter from the other diners
filled my ears.

Vince spoke to me from across the table. He had
wanted to sit next to me, but I said no.

He leaned forward and tried to take my hand.
"Come on, baby, we need to talk."

The only thing I needed was to eat this scrumptious veal scaloppini and escape. Sanity was taking
hold. I understood this was my very own Last
Supper, like Leonardo da Vinci's masterpiece. I
was never doing this again.

But when the waiter came by and asked if we wanted dessert, I couldn't resist tiramisu.

My cell phone rang; I saw Brett was calling me. How could I answer with all this noise around me? And what would I tell him? The truth, that I was having dinner with my former boyfriend, a man I desperately wanted to marry at one time?

"Well?" Vince said. "Why don't you answer? Got a new beau already? I don't see an engagement ring on your left hand,"

I folded my hands in my lap. I had no response, even for myself. I wasn't sure how Brett felt about me. I should have turned off the ringer on the phone. "I'll call back later. We need to finish up here so I can return to my place."

"Are you accepting visitors? I would love to see those flowers."

"I'll text you a photo."

"Oh, come on and give me a break."

"By that, I'm assuming you mean invite you in."

"Would that be so bad?" He massaged his hands together. "You and me, a couple again?"

"Look, I'm going back to Lancaster County in the morning. I need to pack."

"Okay, I hear you. But I want to give you a farewell gift." His hand dipped into his jacket pocket. "I brought you something a little more substantial to remember me by." He pulled his hand out;

I recognized Tiffany's signature blue. I wanted to reach out and touch it but kept my hands clasped in my lap. This turn of events was the last thing I had expected.

"I think we'd better leave," I said.

"Sure, you bet, as soon as you open the box."

What had he bought me? Earrings? A bracelet? The ring I had coveted but never received? I didn't want it, whatever it was. I would not wear it. My sitting here, helping him salve his wounded pride was ludicrous. I should be ashamed of myself.

Now that I thought about it, the Amish didn't even wear wedding rings. Marian wore a simple gold wedding band, and it certainly wasn't from Tiffany's. Her marriage with Sam was the kind I hoped to have someday. So what was I doing here?

"Well, aren't you going to open my gift? I think you'll like it."

"No. I can live with the mystery." Whatever it was would bring me pain.

"How about a little bubbly?" Vince called to the waiter. "Bring us the best champagne in the house."

"A celebration?" the waiter asked with a thick, creamy Italian accent.

"You might say that," Vince said in a booming voice. "I brought this beauty an engagement ring, but she won't even look at it."

A woman at the next table turned to gawk at us. "Go ahead, honey, and open it," she said to me. "I can't wait to get a look."

I realized we had garnered the attention of everyone sitting at the nearby tables, which were so tightly push together I couldn't bolt to my feet or storm out. I was trapped in a most awkward position. But I hadn't lived here my whole life for nothing. I pulled out my best New York City voice.

"I want to leave," I demanded, my voice shrill. "Let me out of here this minute."

The rest of the restaurant grew quiet; all heads rotated my way.

"Okay already," Vince said. "I get the picture." He turned to the other diners and said, "Women. Right?"

Several men chuckled in agreement. Women too.

"Champagne for everyone in the house," he told the waiter. Most in the restaurant cheered.

As I got to my feet, I attempted to look as dignified as possible, but I caught my foot on something and fell forward into Vince's waiting arms.

"This is more like it, baby," he said.

CHAPTER 35

I GRABBED MY COAT off a rack and shoved my hands into the arms as I strode out the door.

"Wait up," Vince called to my departing form. "Let me walk you home. It's not safe out there."

I continued without answering. I listened to his footsteps behind me as I hastened back to my building. Either Vince was following me, or I was about to be mugged. No time to button my coat. I held the front closed and quickened my pace, grasped my purse.

At least this time, the doorman remembered me and tipped his hat. Behind him, I recognized a barking from the foyer. I must be hearing things. No way was my Piper here.

How about a good-night kiss?" Vince asked, catching up with me. I cringed. Nothing was further from my mind. I didn't turn to look at him.

I heard a familiar bark. "Piper? How did you get here, girlie?" I asked my pooch, who was ecstatic to see me. She wasn't supposed to jump, but I couldn't stop her when she was this excited. And I was equally happy to see her. Maybe Vince would fade into the wallpaper and disappear.

"I brought her with me," Brett said, getting up from a chair in the lobby. His jeans and leather jacket were the opposite of Vince's Armani suit and wool coat. "She was miserable without you."

"What are you doing here?" My words came out wrong. I was glad to see Brett, just caught off guard.

"Betsy begged me to bring her to the city. She said she realized too late that she needed to pick up her clothes, too, and then we could give you a ride home at the same time. It seemed like a good idea, but now I realize it wasn't." He looked past me at Vince.

"This isn't what you think it is," I said, my words tripping over themselves.

"Well, aren't you going to introduce us?" Vince squeezed past me and put out his hand to shake Brett's, who took it with reluctance. Brett, I noticed, was several inches taller.

"Any friend of Diana is a friend of mine," Vince said, but Brett didn't answer.

How had I got myself into this tangled mess?

"We were just on our way up to the apartment to see the flowers I sent Diana." Before I could contradict him, Vince pushed the button to open the elevator doors, and Piper pranced right in. I couldn't leave without her.

I said, "Please come up with us, Brett." By *us* I meant Piper and me. I still wasn't looking at Vince or speaking to him. But as soon as I said it, I knew I should have been more specific. Vince had already stepped onto the elevator and selected the correct floor number, proving he knew where I lived. Brett followed, frowning.

"I need to tell Judy to go home without me," I said as the elevator rose. I hated to inconvenience her.

"All taken care of," Brett said. "She said that she was hoping to stay in the city longer, anyway."

"Where will you spend the night?" I asked him.

"At my sister's apartment. Betsy wants to put me to work."

"It will take her mind off the wedding."

"Whose wedding?" Vince asked. "May I escort you, Diana?"

"No. It's in Lancaster County."

"How's that for perfect, since I'm planning to move there? On the weekends, anyway. I could find us a house and meet our new neighbors."

"Vince, it's time for you to go home," I said, as the elevator opened on the seventh floor. "I've got a busy day ahead of me tomorrow."

"Whatever you say, baby. After that fabulous meal and all that champagne, I'm feeling tired myself." He patted his stomach. "Brett and I can ride back down together." Vince gave me an exaggerated wink. I hoped Brett didn't think Vince was coming back to the apartment.

"No, hold on," Vince said, rotating back to the hallway. "I want to see the flowers I sent you." He strode to the door like he owned the place.

Piper wriggled all over me but kept her distance from Vince when he put out his hand to pet her. She had never liked him.

Reluctantly, I followed him to my front door. I couldn't make a scene in the hallway.

Vince removed his jacket and turned it so the Armani label showed. Why had I never seen what a peacock he was? A show-off who was trying to make Brett feel inferior. I was pleased to see Brett was not intimidated in the least. In fact, he said, "Maybe I should stick around too."

"Don't you have livestock and chickens to take care of?" Vince said.

"I would never neglect our animals, especially now that Diana's horse lives with us."

"What?" Vince puffed out his chest, but his muscles that came from machines at the athletic club could not compete with Brett's stature. "No matter what kind of a barn you have, mine will be better."

"As you like. We'll let Diana be the judge." I appreciated Brett's taking the high road. At this moment, I appreciated everything about Brett. As I walked into the apartment's foyer, Vince slipped past me and strode inside. He dipped his hand into his pocket, extracted the Tiffany box and placed it next to the floral bouquet on the table. Vince was certainly persistent.

Brett must have seen it too and surmised its meaning. "On the other hand, I had better be on my way." He glanced at his phone. "I didn't know it was so late."

"It's not so late," I said. "Please stay. Or I'll come with you."

"You're obviously busy." Brett zipped up his jacket and turned away.

"Yes, she is," Vince said. "Glad you could see that."

"Hey, wait a minute." No way was I going to be left alone with Vince. "I thought you were going to ride the elevator down together."

"I'm not getting in the elevator again with that country bumpkin." Vince's voice was filled with distain.

Without a word, Brett stepped into the elevator. The doors swished closed.

"Finally got rid of him," Vince said. "You're way too good for that lowlife."

"Leave this very instant, or I will call security." At the sound of my raised voice, Piper started barking. For once, I wished she would bite him on the ankle.

"But, baby, you haven't opened your present."

"I don't care what's in that box. I don't want it." I stomped my foot for effect. "Take it with you and get out."

"You'll regret this." Vince grabbed the box, shoved it in a pocket.

When Vince departed, I slammed the door and double bolted the lock. Then I tried calling Brett to explain, but he must have turned off his phone.

I unlocked the door and ran to the elevator, but it was stuck on the third floor with an elderly couple entering. I could hear their argument from here. I punched the button with my pointer finger, but no luck summoning the elevator. I dashed to the fire exit and ran down the seven flights.

"Which way did he go?" I asked the doorman, who stared back at me with a blank expression. "The man who just left," I persisted.

"Which one?"

I described Brett, but the doorman said, "I didn't notice."

The sidewalk teamed with pedestrians. Without knowing which direction Brett had taken, I figured following him on foot would be a futile endeavor.

CHAPTER 36

I RAN TO MY cell phone when it chimed the next morning and was disappointed to hear Betsy's voice. "What happened last night?" she asked.

"Just a misunderstanding. May I speak to Brett?"

"Too late, he took off half an hour ago. He's on his way back to Lancaster County without us. He said he left early to avoid the traffic."

Or to avoid me.

"Judy's here and ready to drive both you and me home." I recognized Judy's voice in the background. "Brett at least took most of my stuff in the truck, so there's plenty of room for your clothes in Judy's car."

Despondent is the only word I can use to describe how I felt. I thought about just staying here in Manhattan, but no. Whatever happened with Brett, I was done with city life. My parents would come home from their romantic holiday, and I would be in the way.

Why had I let Brett leave last night? Why hadn't I chased after him all the way to Betsy's place? She'd warned me he shied away from relationships, so I shouldn't be surprised he'd jumped to the wrong conclusion, with Vince acting like a Casanova.

I'd already sorted through my closets and drawers for clothing suitable for Lancaster County. On a whim, I packed an outfit for New Year's Eve, a midi-length forest-green velvet dress with a high neck and billowy long sleeves. I had yet to wear it, because the occasion hadn't arisen, but it suited my new home. No more plunging necklines for this gal. I preferred the simplicity and modesty of dressing plain.

The air outside felt almost like a spring day, practically balmy compared to the frigid cold. I was glad today had warmed, especially since I was worried about an icy welcome when we reached the Yoders' house.

"I feel terrible that I cut your visit short," I told Judy as she exited the highway and started navigating the farm roads of Lancaster County. Much of the snow had melted.

"No matter, my niece can come visit me here." Judy increased her speed to pass a buggy crammed with Amish children.

"They're going to school." Betsy waved at the bearded driver, and he raised a hand in return.

"Not much heating in those buggies, but the children keep warm," Judy said.

It seemed to take forever to reach the Yoders' house. Betsy looked happy to be home. "Better drive us to the back door, okay?"

"You bet." Judy motored around the side of the house, came to a halt. As soon as she set the parking brake, we all piled out. Brett's pickup was nowhere to be seen. My hunch was he'd already left Betsy's stuff here and taken off to avoid me. I felt gloominess encompass me but shook it off as I breathed in the clean and fragrant Lancaster County air. I realized I hadn't fully expanded my lungs since I'd last been here.

Judy helped us unpack. "I'd better scoot," she said. "A couple is waiting for me to take them to the airport."

"Thanks, we're fine, " Betsy said. "We can come back for the rest of the stuff later."

The stairs looked recently swept. Piper and I followed Betsy to the back door. Rex stood inside barking. He and Piper reintroduced themselves, then trotted toward the kitchen. Boxes of Betsy's belongings lined the hallway.

"Come on, girlfriend," Betsy said to me.

"In a minute." Hesitating, I wondered if I'd still be welcomed. What had Brett told them about me, Vince, and the Tiffany box? As I entered the back room, I saw my borrowed slippers. A good sign, I decided. I kicked off my city shoes and stepped into them.

Marian and Sam stood just inside the kitchen. "Perfect timing. Come in." Marian clasped first Betsy, then me in a momentous hug.

"We missed you," she said.

"Both of you," Sam added.

"Am I still welcome?" I asked her.

"Of course you are, honey," Marian said. "For as long as you like. Sam and I were afraid you weren't coming back."

"Here, let me help you." Sam took hold of my largest bag and carried it up the stairs.

I glanced into the living room and noticed the splendid Christmas tree continued to stand. I turned to Marian. "Where's Brett?" I felt awkward saying his name.

"He's helping Jesse." She ushered me to the kitchen table for coffee as Betsy went up to her room with a bag of clothes in each hand. Marian poured me a cup. "I do feel for that boy. Here's a family secret. At the last minute, Sam and I almost didn't get married. In our case, it was me who got cold feet, wondering if I was making a walloping mistake." She brought freshly made blueberry muffins, butter, and plates to the table. I savored a mouthful.

"But I'm guessing you'd rather talk about Brett than hear about me." Her mouth curved into a smile. "He had one steady girlfriend in high school, but she dropped him after the accident. I assume you know about the accident by now."

I nodded. "Yes."

"The girl's parents wouldn't let her go out with him again, not that I blame them. He was driving recklessly." Her smile flattened. "That accident changed his life."

"It sounded horrendous." Too terrible for me to ask for the details. Someday I would hear them. If Brett ever spoke to me again.

"I bet you want to visit Misty." Sam strolled past us. "Care to come on out to the barn with me, Diana? You know the drill. Grab any jacket and boots you fancy."

"Thanks." I wanted to hear more, but I also needed to start taking care of my own horse. I left my coffee and half the muffin. "I'll be back."

In my excitement, I trotted ahead of Sam. Inside the barn, the aroma was heavenly.

"Misty, do you remember me?" Her ears bent forward as I neared her.

"Want to take her out for a ride?" Sam asked me.

I had imagined Brett would be the first person to take me riding, but I knew I could trust Sam.

"It's been years," I said. "But if you help me bridle and saddle her, I'll give it a try."

"First she needs grooming. Always groom before and after you ride." He handed me a brush, and I began my slow methodical chore, which turned out to be a joyful bonding experience.

"Next goes the blanket. I'll do it this time, and let Brett give you a lesson later, when he gets home."

"If he comes home, with me here," I muttered.

Sam gave me a quizzical look. "You two have a spat?"

Where to start? "An old boyfriend showed up and tried to come between us." I watched Sam cinch on the saddle. "I went out to dinner with him at an Italian joint a block from my apartment building. But Vince—that's his name—made a big deal out of it. I never should have gone. I could kick myself."

He winced. "That sounds painful."

"It was." I was amazed Brett had not lost his temper. If he had decked Vince, I wouldn't have blamed him. But that didn't seem to be the Mennonite way.

"Brett's a big boy," Sam said. "If he cares for you, don't make things too easy for him when he comes back." He adjusted Misty's bridle. "Would you like to pay Jesse a visit? The land between our houses is still pretty soggy, but you might enjoy seeing how his barn is coming along."

"I would, very much." Standing on Misty's left side, I inserted my foot in the stirrup and pulled myself up. I was surprised how nervous I was.

"I'll lead you and Misty up our lane to the main road and then down to Jesse's farm."

"That would be great."

"Prepare yourself to be amazed by how much has changed in only two days. The whole community pitched in to help."

"Still no clues on how the fire started?"

"The fire marshal has been questioning everyone, even Marian and me. Wanted to know, did we see anyone unusual?"

"Well, did you?"

"Only that rapscallion Tommy. But just because he has an abrasive personality does not make him an arsonist."

"Abrasive is a kind way of putting it. I heard him coming on to Naomi."

He glanced up at me. "We must not gossip."

"You're right." Tommy was a prince compared to smooth-talking Vince.

"Marian and I got to chatting with the fire marshal over coffee. He let slip that they have a suspect in York County west of here. He said most barn fires are caused by an arsonist." He chuckled. "You know how good Marian's muffins are. The man was in no hurry to leave."

"Maybe a kerosine lantern got tipped over somehow. Or faulty wiring?"

"No electrical wiring," he said. "And I doubt Jesse uses kerosine lanterns anymore. Some Old Order Amish use diesel oil, which is flammable. But I've never been in his barn."

We reached the roadway. I heard the clip-clopping of a horse pulling a buggy. What a glorious sound.

Sam led Misty down Jesse's lane. "Would you like me to let go of the reins now?"

I hated to admit how timid I was. "Not yet."

"You two will have plenty of time to get to know each other. No hurry."

"Thanks, I appreciate your patience."

As we approached Jesse's home, a dozen crows took off, filling the air with sounds of fluttering wings and cawing. Misty, spooked, reared back and pulled the reins out of Sam's hand. I instinctively leaned forward and grabbed her mane, using my knees to stay in the saddle. I can do this, I said to myself as I recalled my instructors' lessons. But then I felt my rear end raising off the saddle and flying in slow motion, landing on the ground.

Sam hollered for Brett and Jesse, who must have been watching out the window because I heard their running footsteps soon after. I felt mostly embarrassed, though there was a stab of pain in my left shoulder and hip. Unsure what to do next, I lay on the snowy ground, gazing up at the blue sky and watching the crows retreat into the bare trees.

"Darling," Brett said to me. "Can you hear me? Are you okay?"

Had he just called me *darling*? Apparently, he wasn't mad at me anymore. "Promise you'll stay here with me forever." He brought my fingertips to his lips. "That you won't marry that Vince fellow."

"No," I said. "I won't. Only you." Had I just answered an unasked question?

"Seriously, Diana? You'd marry me?"

"Yes, if you asked."

EPILOGUE

Enticing my parents to leave the city to attend my and Brett's wedding was like getting Tommy to join the Amish church, which in fact he finally did.

"Mennonite?" Mom had asked with a squawk. "What kind of a church is that? We have so many splendid cathedrals on Manhattan Island. Couldn't you get married in one of those and then have a big to-do after? Champagne caviar. The works." It took a while, but she finally realized I wasn't going to give in to her, not even with a fabulous restaurant catering and ritzy venues that Lancaster County could not hold a candle to. None of that mattered to me anymore.

"Wait a year," my father had advised me. Mom echoed his sentiments. I knew it was good and prudent advice, but I'd already waited a lifetime to be cherished and adored by a man I loved. Lingering until June was hard enough. Buds burst in the trees, and flowers bloomed in Amish gardens.

I begged Mom not to wear anything too glitzy to our ceremony, but my request was a lost cause. She arrived bejeweled in the highest of heels and the flashy pastel-blonde mink swing coat she saved for gala occasions like opening night at the opera. Her hair had been professionally coifed for the occasion, swept back to reveal the aquamarine earrings and the necklace Dad gave her. My parents still acted like a couple of lovebirds.

For fun, Brett and I arrived at the church in a horse and buggy, lent to us and driven by Jesse, now a married man himself and growing a beard. I was relieved Midnight didn't run away with us onboard. The stallion had settled down somewhat, but only Jesse could control him—most of the time. I smiled when I recalled his and Naomi's wedding. I'd been warned about the hard seats, but there was no way around them. Bishop Harold officiated what seemed like a regular church service with Jesse and Naomi exchanging vows at the end. No nonsense Harold had used scripture to speak of the sanctity of marriage. Naomi, in a cornflower-blue dress and her heart-shaped head covering, had beamed with euphoria, but Jesse had worn the expression

of a man being sentenced to life imprisonment—
until the end, when all the seats were rearranged
and stuffed chicken was served.

Diana scanned the room of about three-hundred Amish guests. Her vision honed in on the
unusual centerpieces perched on the tables: mason
jars stuffed with celery stalks instead of flowers.
Except for the many wedding cakes needed to feed
over three-hundred people, was there a food dish
that didn't include celery?

Once seated at the corner table with his bride,
Jesse regained his composure and grinned, acting
as though marrying Naomi had been his intention
all along.

Today, Jesse is Brett's best man at our wedding,
and Betsy is my maid of honor. Naomi, Jesse's wife
of four months, sits with her father, the bishop.
Sam, Marian, Brett's sisters, and Jesse's many relatives fill the first rows of the progressive Mennonite church.

The church is standing room only, but I must
keep my focus on Brett.

My attire? Much to my mother's chagrin, I chose
to keep things simple instead of the elaborate bridal
dresses Mom suggested. For months she'd sent me
pictures torn out of magazines and had offered to
pay for the gown of my choice. Instead, I wear the

dress Marian sewed: an ivory jewel-neck satin gown with a modest lace head covering.

My mother thought I'd really lost my mind when I told her Piper would serve as our ring bearer. Even the pastor asked about my choice. Were we sure? Could the dog be trusted not to swallow the ring? But when I explained how Piper had helped save Melvin and Jesse during the barn fire, he smiled and said, "Good job, little dog."

As the pastor conducts the service, I glance into the congregation and see my mother dabbing under her eyes. She looks elated. I know her well enough to read her emotions.

Brett follows the pastor's lead. "I take you, Diana, to be my wife . . ." Brett's voice is filled with emotion. "I will respect, trust, help, and care for you . . ."

When it's my turn, I hold in my tears of joy. "I, Diana . . . promise to share my life with you." Gazing into Brett's face, my words feel stuck in my throat, but I manage to say what is in my heart. "I will be faithful to you and honest with you . . . through the best and the worst of what is to come."

Out of my peripheral vision, I see Brett's family grinning, Except Marian, who dabs under her eyes. I understand that she is also delighted.

"As long as you both shall live," the pastor says. "Brett, you may kiss your bride."

Have I ever been happier?

Brett leans down to bestow a tender kiss on my lips that sends a thrill through me. I long for more. He whispers in my ear, "I'll love you from now and forever."

Then we turn to the congregation. Cheers, well-wishes, and laughter fill the sanctuary as we hold hands and stroll down the center aisle—a bounce in each step.

MARIAN'S CHICKEN POTPIE RECIPE

INGREDIENTS:

1 1/2 pounds boneless chicken breast or tenders or thighs

Note: you may use 3 cups of shredded cooked chicken instead

1/2 teaspoon sage

1/4 teaspoon oregano

Salt and a pinch of pepper

4 tablespoons butter

1/2 cup finely diced onion

1/2 cup diced celery

1 cup frozen peas and carrots, thawed

1/4 cup flour

3 cups chicken broth

1/4 teaspoon turmeric

Additional salt and pepper, to taste

Chopped fresh thyme to taste

1/4 cup milk (or half-and-half for a richer, creamier pie)

1 unbaked pie crust (homemade or store bought)

1 whole egg

2 tablespoons water

DIRECTIONS:

1. Preheat oven to 400 degrees.
2. Sprinkle the chicken breast with the sage, oregano, salt, and pepper. Melt the butter in a large pot over medium-high heat. Add seasoned chicken breast and sauté until cooked through. Remove chicken from pan, let rest a few minutes, and cut into bite-size cubes.
3. Add the onion and celery to the same pan, adding a pat more butter if needed, and cook until translucent, about 3 minutes.
4. Stir in the cooked and chopped chicken, peas, and carrots. Sprinkle the flour over the top, and stir it until combined. Cook for 1 minute, then pour in the chicken broth. Stir to combine, and cook until it thickens.

5. Add turmeric, salt, pepper, and thyme. Add the milk (or half-and-half). Stir to combine, and cook until it thickens, about 4 minutes.

6. Pour the filling into a 2-quart baking dish. Roll out the pie crust on a floured surface (store bought okay), and lay it over the top of the dish. Press the dough so that the edges stick to the outside of the pan. Use a knife to cut vents into the crust.

7. Mix together the egg with 2 tablespoons water, and brush over the surface of the crust. (There will be some left over.)

8. Place the pie on a rimmed baking sheet, and bake for 25 to 30 minutes, until the crust is deep golden brown and the filling is bubbly. To prevent the crust from getting too brown, you may want to cover it lightly with foil halfway through baking.

ACKNOWLEDGEMENTS

I AM GRATEFUL to my many readers, who send encouraging letters, emails, and interact with me on Facebook and Instagram. A huge shout-out to those who post online reviews and those supporting me on my Review Crew!

Thank you to my friend and encourager Mary Jackson. To fellow author Kathleen Kohler. To bestselling Old Order Amish novelist Linda Byler, author of *Banished*, who patiently answers my questions. Thank you to Marian Roberts and her son, Mark Roberts. Thank you, Lisa-Ann Oliver of Web Designs by LAO, the best webmaster an author could have. Thanks to my sister, Margaret Coppock, who helps me with grammar and a host of questions, and to her husband, Don, who helped copy edit my manuscript. Thank you, Herb Scrivener, for sharing your Lancaster County expertise and continuing to answer the phone when you see my number appear on caller ID. Mega thanks to Hillary Manton Lodge for my fabulous cover. Thank you to my most excellent publishing consultant, Beth Jusino. Thanks, Piper, my loyal and sweet Cairn terrier, who agreed to be a character in this book.

ABOUT THE AUTHOR

A NATIVE OF Baltimore, Kate Lloyd lives with her husband in Seattle, WA. She adores spending time with friends and family in Lancaster County, Pennsylvania, the inspiration for *A Lancaster Family Christmas*, as well as her bestselling novels *Leaving Lancaster*, *Pennsylvania Patchwork*, *Forever Amish*, *A Letter from Lancaster County*, and *Starting from Scratch*.

Kate studied art, art history, and photography in college. She loved living in Rome. She has worked a variety of jobs, including restaurateur and car salesman. Kate is a member of the Lancaster Mennonite Historical Society. Kate enjoys reading Christmas books all year round, travel, and walking her sweet Cairn terrier, Piper.

Find out more about Kate Lloyd:
Website: www.katelloyd.com
Blog: http://katelloyd.com/blog/
Facebook: www.facebook.com/katelloydbooks
Instagram: katelloydauthor
Pinterest: @KateLloydAuthor

Kate loves hearing from readers!

Discussion Questions

1. Which character do you identify with the most and why?

2. How did Diana's parents' contentious marriage affect her relationships with men? Have your parents adversely or positively affected your relationships?

3. When it comes to travel, are you spontaneous or cautious, wanting to ponder the details? Would you have hopped in the car with Betsy and driven to Lancaster County on the spur of the moment?

4. How does harboring unforgiveness affect a person? What is the best way to rid yourself of the burden of clinging onto resentment? How does holding a grudge hurt you more than the other person, who may not even know you are angry?

5. Do you admire Jesse and the Amish community for forgiving Brett? How would you have dealt with your grief and sense of loss?

6. Which man do you find more attractive and why?

7. Have you ever wanted to reinvent your life, including a new job, a significant move, or change in lifestyle? What is stopping you?